BULBURY KNAP

BULBURY KNAP

Sheila Spencer-Smith

CHIVERS

British Library Cataloguing in Publication Data available

This Large Print edition published by BBC Audiobooks Ltd, Bath, 2009.
Published by arrangement with the Author.

U.K. Hardcover ISBN 978 1 408 44210 4
U.K. Softcover ISBN 978 1 408 44211 1

Printed and bound in Great Britain by
CPI Antony Rowe, Chippenham and Eastbourne

CHAPTER ONE

Kathryn, long hair swinging, turned from the open window of the small flat to check that her mother's belongings were all on the bed waiting to be packed.

'Why the sigh?' asked Sarah briskly.

Behind Kathryn the London traffic roared. She shut the window with a bang and at once the sound was muffled. 'Oh Mum, Bulbury Knap is such a long way away. Are you sure you're doing the right thing?'

Sarah, busy folding clothes and placing them in her suitcase, looked supremely confident. 'Of course, love. Haven't I said so a thousand times?'

Kathryn smiled, though her mouth felt stiff. 'A hundred at least,' she admitted. This was not the moment to voice lingering doubts about this place, Bulbury Knap. What if it was a complete dump, run down and impossible for one person to cope with? Mum hadn't even seen it, for goodness' sake, or met her prospective employers. Charming as this great-nephew sounded from what Mum said when he interviewed her on their behalf he wasn't going to be at Bulbury Knap all the time. And why the haste in getting her down to Dorset? Suppose there was some dark reason for his hurry?

1

But it was too late to change anything now and all she could do was help clear up the flat and offer to see Mum safely on to the coach for the West Country.

'I still can't get my head round it,' said Kathryn. 'It's all happened so quickly. One minute you're working for your old lady, the next she's whisked off to a residential home by her family leaving you jobless. Then you're heading out of London to work in a place miles away from anywhere.'

'Stop worrying, love,' Sarah said gently. 'Think how lovely the countryside will look now it's springtime. And Sir Edwin and Lady Hewson sound charming people from what the nephew said. They're anxious to stay in their own place and just need somebody to keep an eye on them and see to the house.' She closed the lid of her suitcase and zipped it up with a flourish. 'There, that's done. And we've plenty of time for a cuppa before you drive me to the coach station.'

As they sat side by side in the living room drinking tea, Kathryn began at last to be affected with her mother's enthusiasm. Bulbury Knap was in a part of the country where Mum's father had been evacuated to as a child during the Second World War. He'd taken his family on holiday there. The place had memories for Mum, for goodness' sake. Of course it was the right thing for her to do.

'I'm not the only employee down at Bulbury

Knap,' Sarah said. 'There's an estate manager who looks after the grounds, Michael Carey by name. A bit of a bossy boots from what the nephew said.'

'They don't get on?'

Sarah frowned. 'It seems not. The nephew doesn't like him, for sure. He didn't say why but he gave a strong impression he'd like to give him his marching orders. But Michael's well in with Sir Edwin apparently. Takes him about a bit. Lady Hewson likes him too.'

'Intriguing.'

Sarah shrugged. 'Oh well, the house will be my province and there'll be plenty there to keep me occupied. I'm looking forward to it.'

'Does this Michael Carey live in?'

'The nephew was very cagey when it came to talking about him so I didn't pursue it. I'll find out soon enough, I expect.'

Kathryn got up and collected the mugs to carry them through to the kitchen.

'Sir Edwin and Lady Hewson open the place to the public during the summer months, I gather,' said Sarah, following her and picking up a tea towel.

'What?'

'The house, Bulbury Knap.'

'They do?'

'Garden clubs mostly. As well as looking round the grounds the members get the run of the house too. I'll enjoy that. It'll be interesting meeting people.'

3

'Of course it will,' Kathryn said. 'I'm pleased for you, Mum, really I am. They're going to be lucky having you as their housekeeper.'

*   *   *

Kathryn's eyes were moist as the coach turned the corner and she could see it no more.

Feeling suddenly bereft, she headed for the nearest café. She needed time to come to terms with Mum's departure before returning to the flat to check that all was in order for the next tenant.

Seated at a table in the window, she clicked on her mobile and rang her sister's number. To her surprise her brother-in-law answered. 'Dan? Is anything wrong?'

'Helen's in bed, feeling a bit under the weather. Nothing to worry about.' His voice sounded anxious and far away.

Well, Cornwall was far away. Not so far from Dorset, though, where Mum was heading. One of the bonuses for Sarah taking the job was to be nearer her pregnant daughter.

'Helen's going to be all right?'

'Asleep, I think, or you could talk to her. I'll get her to ring you back. The doctor says everything's fine. Just has to take life easy with no worries.'

'You're at home at the moment?'

'I've got the afternoon off so I can meet

4

Jamie from school. A good thing the weekend's coming up. She'll be fine, Kathryn.'

'Could you tell her I've just seen Mum off on the coach for Dorset?'

'Will do. Take care.'

'You too, Dan. I'll be in touch.'

Later, Kathryn unlocked the door of her own flat with a feeling of relief. She would have a shower and get herself down to the restaurant to spend the evening in Nick's company. This wasn't one of her nights for working there but it would be good to see him.

Eyes closed, she let the warm water flow over her body. Kathryn smiled. Letting the strain of these last few days stream away was wonderful.

At last she stepped out and reached for her bath sheet, rubbing herself dry with increasing vigour so that her skin glowed. Since she wasn't due to be working in the restaurant this evening she chose to wear her new jeans with a soft olive-green top, her colour of the moment.

She went downstairs. *The Green Walnut Tree* wasn't busy tonight. Good, that meant Nick, as owner-manager, wouldn't be heavily involved and perhaps not busy at all. Some of the tables were occupied but most were still in their pristine condition waiting for diners who might come later or might not come at all. She and Nick would have time to talk and catch up on things.

Kathryn pushed open the door and went

inside. Soft classical music floating in the warm air and the murmur of voices were welcoming. She saw the flash of green and white as one of the waitresses vanished through the serving door, a hint of roast lamb aroma floating into the room as she did so. Bella, the new waitress, greeted her.

'Seen Nick about?' Kathryn asked.

Bella hesitated, glancing swiftly at the door that led into the passage on the other side of the room. 'Nick's not here,' she said.

Kathryn smiled at her. Not quite the question she had asked, but never mind. She walked across the room to the door at the far side. This led to Nick's office and a couple of the rooms used for storage.

She heard the voices as she walked down the passage. Afterwards she thought she should have been warned, but nothing prepared her for the shock when she opened the office door.

'Nick!' she cried, her voice strangled. She should have kept quiet, crept out of the room again and pretended she had seen nothing. That way she could have walked back through the restaurant, smiling at Bella with her pride intact.

Nick and Anna sprang apart.

Even then Kathryn's mind couldn't quite take in what she was seeing. She was unable to move for the time it took Anna to button her white blouse and straighten her skirt.

Kathryn raised her eyes and looked at Nick. Suddenly she could see exactly how it was, how it had been between him and his head waitress for some weeks past. Often there had been a certain stillness between the two of them, a feeling of communication without anything being said that hadn't disturbed Kathryn at the time but she now knew was significant. She should have known.

*   *   *

The phone rang.

Nick of course, Kathryn let it ring but then could stand it no longer and rushed to pick up the receiver.

'We've got to talk,' he said, his voice hoarse.

She almost laughed and the sound came out as a strangled sob. 'How long has this been going on, Nick?'

'I can't leave the restaurant at the moment,' he said.

Well no, she supposed he couldn't but where did that leave her? No way was she going to return to *The Green Walnut Tree* and see Bella's pitying looks. How long had Bella known, had everybody known except herself? She imagined them talking about her, wondering what Nick had seen in her when the gorgeous Anna was working with him in close proximity five days a week. Now they would know he had thought her gorgeous too.

'Stay there,' he ordered. 'I'll come when we close.'

And when would that be, midnight? She had a teaching job tomorrow. 'I'm going to bed,' she said. 'I've an early start in the morning.'

'Don't you want us to get this sorted out?'

'What is there to sort out?' she asked crisply. 'It's finished between us, Nick. I can see that. Finished.' She managed to get the last word out without breaking down but it was a struggle. Not wanting to risk her voice any more, she put the phone down and then stood with her hand pressing on the receiver as if she expected it to bob up again.

He didn't try to ring again and Kathryn knew he would wait until tomorrow and then come up with some excellent excuse for what had happened. An unpaid navvy, that's what she had been, helping out in *The Green Walnut Tree* whenever she could. What a fool. But not any more.

*   *   *

Kathryn woke late. She was due at Meadowland Primary at eight-thirty and it was now eight o'clock. She tried not to panic as she grabbed her clothes and threw them on. No time for even a cup of tea. She had to hit the road immediately. She hated cutting it fine like this but at least it gave her no time to think of the events of yesterday evening. Her personal feelings must remain hidden for the time being for the sake of the children she would be with today.

Head held high, she walked through the noisy playground and entered the building.

There were times during the busy day when the agony threatened to surface in spite of her resolve and the effort of keeping it hidden was acute. She wondered that no one noticed.

When at last she was free to leave she almost ran out of the building to reach the seclusion of her car, glad that the traffic was heavy and the drive home needed all her attention. She half-dreaded that Nick would be on the doorstep waiting for her, but there was no-one there. He would come later, she was sure, but in the meantime she would have something to eat and drink and fortified, be prepared to stand her ground and finish with him.

The bell rang at eight o'clock. Kathryn pressed the button to release the lock on the outside door and waited, heart thudding. Nick came in slowly and looked pale as she felt she did herself. His usual immaculate look had gone and in its place was a scruffy stranger she no longer wanted anything to do with.

'I can explain,' he said when he reached her.

'No *way*,' she said. 'I'm glad I've found out at last. There's nothing to be said, Nick. I don't want to see you again, ever. This is how it is.'

9

He said nothing. Had he tried to persuade her to change her mind she might have succumbed. As it was she just wished he would go away and leave her alone. When he did, at last, she went at once to bed, glad to hide her head beneath the duvet and give herself up to grief for the loss of someone she thought had cared.

Much later she woke with a start. It was dark now and still windy. She switched on the bedside lamp. She hadn't heard from Mum to say she'd arrived safely at Bulbury Knap. She looked at her watch. Five minutes past midnight.

Maybe Mum had phoned Helen but it was too late now to check. In any case it might not be a *good* idea to worry Helen if she hadn't. No doubt there was some simple explanation.

Early next morning Kathryn telephoned Bulbury Knap. The ringing tone seemed to go on for ever. No answerphone there then. Maybe Mum was working in another part of the house out of earshot. Odd, though. You would think that since bookings would have to be taken for visiting groups that several telephones would be strategically placed throughout the building. Surprising that Mum hadn't got this organised already.

The receiver was picked up at the other end with a crackling sound. No one said anything.

'May I speak to Mrs Sarah Marshall?' Kathryn said. 'I'm her daughter phoning from

10

London,'

A gasp came down the line and the sound of some muttering.

Startled, Kathryn spoke more sharply than she intended. 'Is everything all right?'

A quavering male voice answered her. 'Who did you say you were, my dear?'

This was worrying. Unless he was hard of hearing and hadn't picked up what she had said. In that case why was he answering the telephone?

'I'm Mrs Marshall's daughter,' she said loudly and slowly. 'Is my mother there? Can I speak to her, please?'

'Well no, my dear. I'm afraid that's not possible.'

'Not possible?'

'I regret I'm not able to grant your request at the present moment.'

The voice on the other end sounded faint now and she had difficulty in picking up what he was saying. With a jolt she realised she was probably speaking to Sir Edwin Hewson of Bulbury Knap himself. She took a deep breath. 'Is there anyone there who could tell me?'

'I'm so sorry, my dear. This is a bad line. I'm speaking from Bulbury Knap, Edwin Hewson. How can I help you?'

'My mother, Mrs Marshall . . .'

'We haven't seen Mrs Marshall,' Sir Edwin said, suddenly loud and clear.

The receiver trembled in Kathryn's hand.

11

'You mean, my mother didn't arrive at Bulbury Knap on Thursday?'

'No, my dear,' he said. 'Mrs Marshall didn't arrive when she was expected and there was no message.'

Kathryn replaced the receiver. Her instinct was to jump in the car immediately and head for Dorset but there were phone calls to be made first. Should she notify the police?

Early as it was Helen would be having breakfast with young Jamie in far-away Cornwall. She must take care not to alarm her sister too much at this stage.

She tried her mother's mobile again. There was no response.

CHAPTER TWO

Kathryn had memorised the way she should go when it was time to turn off the A35 but somehow the narrow high-banked Dorset lane was bending the wrong way. Her impulsiveness in rushing down to the West Country was likely to get her into trouble if she wasn't careful. She was making a poor show in solving the mystery stuck here in this horribly remote place.

Suppose she hadn't done the right thing, as well, in keeping Helen in the dark? How fair was that? At least she had contacted the police before she left even though they hadn't got back in touch with her yet. She had phoned the coach company, too, but no suitcase had been handed in to lost property. Had Mum simply failed to get back on the coach after one of the stops?

She came to a crossroads and slowed to read the unfamiliar place names. They were no help at all unless she consulted her road atlas. She drew into a gateway and pulled the map out. Before she could open it she became aware that a vehicle had pulled up alongside her, a four-wheel drive that completely blocked the lane.

The driver wound down the window on her side and ran his hand through his mop of fair hair.

'Can I help?' he asked, his voice deep and reassuring.

She opened her window too. 'I'm looking for a place called Bulbury Knap,' she said. 'Near Willowdown.'

His eyes narrowed. 'Bulbury Knap?'

'Yes,' said Kathryn. 'Well, that is . . . I'm looking for my mother.'

'She didn't give you the precise directions?'

'She couldn't.' Her voice wavered as she sensed his obvious suspicion. 'It's . . . it's not her fault. I'm Kathryn Marshall.'

He nodded and she saw recognition dawn. 'Ah, Mrs Marshall, the new housekeeper?'

'You've met my mother?' Hope rose and

then was as quickly dashed.

'I've been away for a few days. Are you expected?'

'I think so. I don't know. She didn't arrive at Bulbury Knap and I don't know where she is.' To Kathryn's horror her lips trembled.

'But you've spoken to Sir Edwin?' His tone was matter of fact.

She gulped and nodded. 'I thought the best thing was to come down but now I'm lost.'

He cast a severe look at her. 'So you've travelled all the way down from London to find her when you know she's not at Bulbury Knap?'

Put like that it sounded irresponsible and she could see that he thought so by his frown. 'I had to come. I'm so worried. I saw her on the coach on Thursday, you see, and there's been no word from her.'

'Well follow me. It's not far.'

There was a loud tooting from behind and at once his vehicle sprang to life and he moved on. Letting the car behind pass, Kathryn followed. There was nothing else to do in her predicament. The lane twisted and turned, passing road junctions half-hidden behind high hedges.

At last she found herself driving behind him down a narrow high-banked lane. A sharp turn left took them into an unfenced drive. The expanse of grass on either side was dotted with huge bare-branched oak trees. At the bottom

14

Kathryn saw a house of warm stone whose mullioned windows gleamed in the sunshine.

He flashed his lights and indicated she should park in front of the house next to his vehicle. Opening the car door she got out. He had already pulled the chain at the side of the front door and the jangling of the bell echoed inside the house. At last the door swung open and an elderly gentleman stood there looking at her beneath heavy brows.

She felt her rescuer's hand on her shoulder. 'This is Mrs Marshall's daughter, Sir Edwin,' he said in his deep voice. And to her, 'I'll leave you now but I'm not far away if any help is needed.'

'Miss Marshall?' Sir Edwin looked frail as he leaned on his walking stick and she felt a moment's compassion for an old man being thrown into a worrying situation through no fault of his own. His courteous manner was charming as he indicated that she should come inside.

A slight sound made her look round at someone who could only be Lady Hewson. Wispy hair clung to her small head and the sweet expression on her face turned to one of concern as she clasped Kathryn's hand. 'I'm so glad you've come, dear,' she said simply. 'Did Edwin tell you that we had a phone call?'

'From my mother?' Kathryn felt relief flood her like a warm tide.

Sir Edwin cleared his throat. 'We had a

15

message to say that Mrs Marshall has been retained in hospital.'

'In hospital?' Kathryn couldn't help a little quiver in her voice. 'But why?'

'Come into the den, my dear,' Lady Hewson said. 'And please, don't worry.'

The den was a cosy room off the hall where a small fire burned in the grate in spite of the warm sunshine outside. Several rather battered chairs stood about.

'Do take a seat,' Lady Hewson invited in a gentle voice.

They were a delightful couple, one so upright and white-haired and the other a little shaky and so thin she looked as if she could be blown away by the slightest breath of air. Sir Edwin made sure his wife was comfortable and then, giving a little grunt, lowered himself into a high-backed chair. 'We were told that her daughter would be in touch with us in due course,' he said when he was settled.

'No one has told me anything,' said Kathryn.

Lady Hewson leaned forward and patted Kathryn's hand. 'That's all we know, dear. Maybe you should telephone the hospital now.'

Kathryn pulled out her mobile.

'The telephone is along the passage,' said Sir Edwin gruffly. 'We have no mobile signal here, I'm afraid.'

'The hills, you see, dear,' said Lady Hewson.

16

'You'll find the number on the pad.'

Kathryn sprang up. 'Thank you.' Hurrying from the room, she located the phone. A few moments later she was speaking to the staff nurse of Cheney Ward but her heart was thumping so much it was hard to hear.

'We've been trying to contact you, my dear. We think you should come.'

'But what happened? Why is my mother in hospital? Did she have an accident?'

'The car she was in . . . a collision. She's regained consciousness . . .'

'I'll be there as soon as I can.' The room began to spin as Kathryn replaced the receiver. Car . . . what car?

Sir Edwin struggled to his feet as Kathryn returned to the den.

'I still don't know what happened,' she said, struggling to keep her voice steady. 'I'm sorry you've had all this worry.'

Lady Hewson gazed at her with sympathy. Sir Edwin cleared his throat and his hand trembled on his walking stick.

Kathryn's heart went out to them, so proud and trail but so obviously full of concern for her. 'I must go at once,' she said gently. 'But where's the hospital? I didn't ask.'

'A few miles away,' said Sir Edwin. 'If you wait just a moment I'll arrange some transport.'

'Edwin will get Michael to take you in,' said Lady Hewson as her husband left the room.

'He won't be long.'

Michael Carey? Mum had said something about him and Kathryn wasn't sure about this. 'I can drive myself,' she said.

'Nonsense, dear. It's no trouble for Michael.'

On a low table near the window stood a photograph in an ornate frame. As Lady Hewson saw Kathryn glance in that direction she got up from her chair and picked it up. 'This is Edwin's great-nephew, Andrew,' she said proudly as she held it so that Kathryn could see. 'Don't you think he's handsome?'

Kathryn stared at the photograph, willing herself to concentrate on what Lady Hewson was saying. The face seemed to be smiling directly at her and the brown eyes sparkled as if at a shared joke. He was wearing an open-necked crimson shirt that set off the mass of dark curly hair that framed his good-looking face.

'Such a shame you couldn't meet Andrew today,' Lady Hewson murmured as they heard the four-wheel drive drawing up on the gravel drive outside.

Michael Carey swung his long legs out of the vehicle. He had changed the light T-shirt he had been wearing earlier for a deep blue sweatshirt that made his eyes look very blue in his tanned face.

He held open the passenger door for her and made sure she was settled before moving

18

off.

'I could have driven myself,' she said as they left the drive and travelled up the lane. 'But I don't know where the hospital is.'

'Then it's as well I do,' he said.

Kathryn was silent, unsure of what to say next. This was the man the Hewsons' great nephew wanted out. Bossy, the nephew had told Mum, implying a lot more that a few days ago she had thought merely intriguing. Now it was important to know why. She glanced at his large hands on the steering wheel. They seemed capable, strong.

The cuff of his sweatshirt was frayed in one place as if he'd caught it on a nail or something. Perhaps he'd been putting up some trellis or knocking nails into the garden wall to tie up straying roses. 'Or honeysuckle,' she said out loud.

'Honeysuckle?'

'Sorry, I was thinking.'

'Nice thoughts to have.'

'Not at all.'

He shot her a sideways amused glance. 'Do you often think of flowers?'

'Flowers?'

'Coloured things on the end of stems. Sweetly scented some of them.'

She laughed.

'That's better,' he said. 'Sir Edwin told me about your mother. She won't want to see you looking so strained when she regains

19

consciousness.'

All at once she knew she could trust him. 'I know,' she said. 'But there's so much I don't understand.'

'You'll find out very soon.'

She would, of course. Suddenly she needed to talk, to tell this kind man all that had happened since the shock of losing her job and, obviously, her home. Without going into much detail, and keeping Nick right out of it, she told him a little of what had been happening. Stop it. She was babbling too much.

To her relief she saw that they were arriving on the outskirts of town at last. Together they walked in the main door of the hospital. 'This *way,*' Michael said with authority, leading the way to the reception desk.

Kathryn was glad to have his company as they found their way to Cheney Ward on the first floor.

'Ah yes, Mrs Marshall,' the young nurse said kindly. 'Your mother was unconscious when they brought her in on Thursday.'

'Can I see her?'

'Of course. But we allow only two visitors and there's someone with her.'

Kathryn gazed at her uncomprehendingly. 'Someone with her?'

'I'll go into town and get a bite to eat,' Michael said. 'I've some business to do. I'll return and wait for you in due course. Sir

Edwin's orders.'

For a moment Kathryn stood in the doorway of the side ward staring at the immobile figure in the bed wired up to some sort of machine and with a drip close to one side. Then she went forward and bent to kiss her mother, hardly able to speak for the tears in her throat at seeing how white and still she was. 'Mum, oh, Mum!' she cried.

She became aware of a large form in a white hospital gown seated in a wheelchair on the other side of the bed. A dark bruise stained one cheek. 'Zillah?' she gasped. 'Is it really you?'

'Oh Kathryn, I'm so sorry. You'll kill me. I know you will. It's all my fault.'

Kathryn hesitated, bemused. That husky voice was a familiar one, a voice she had grown up with, her best friend from nursery school days. But how could this be? Kathryn's head spun. She hadn't heard from Zillah for months.

'I'm living at Lyme now,' Zillah murmured. 'We met in the café at Bridport, your mum and me. I offered her a lift. There was an accident . . . ' Her voice broke and she fumbled in her loose gown for a tissue.

Hours later Kathryn staggered out of the main hospital door, knowing that Michael Carey was waiting for her because he had sent in a message as she sat by her mother's bed. She had hardly moved in all that time except

21

to come outside and make some phone calls. One was to leave a message on Helen's answerphone. Another was to the police to say she had found her mother in hospital.

'Mum, Mum,' she had whispered as her mother first stirred and opened her eyes.

'Kathryn?' Sarah whispered.

It seemed as if a light had suddenly been switched on. 'It's me,' said Kathryn, swallowing a lump in her throat.

Michael Carey was waiting for her in the reception area as he had promised. On seeing his familiar figure, huge in his blue sweatshirt, Kathryn ran to him. 'Oh Michael,' she cried.

His arms went round her and as she collapsed against him in a huge lessening of tension. For a moment she allowed herself the luxury of letting go but then she struggled to control her tears. She pulled away, taking deep breaths. 'She's sleeping peacefully now,' she said brokenly. 'They said I should leave and get some rest and get back there in the morning.'

They walked to the Land Rover. Kathryn leaned back in her seat and closed her eyes. 'A broken ankle, severe bruising,' she said as Michael reversed out of the parking space in the gathering dusk. 'A car accident. She had a lift. Someone drove straight out at a road junction at them and now the car's a write-off.'

Kathryn shuddered as she imagined the scene, police and ambulance summoned, sirens blaring. And poor Mum in the middle of it all, unconscious, and no-one knowing how to get hold of her. 'There was no identification, no bag because it's gone missing. The friend she was with, Zillah, told them about my boyfriend's restaurant in Wimbledon and the hospital left a message. But I never got it.'

'I see,' Michael said as they joined a stream of traffic.

She glanced at him and saw his jaw set hard as he gazed straight ahead. He couldn't really know how it was, no one could. When, earlier, she had dialled *The Green Walnut Tree* number to ask why the message hadn't been passed on she hadn't expected Nick to be available and was surprised to hear his gravelly voice.

Taking in what he was saying about a temporary waitress messing things up and losing the paper on which she had written it down was hard. It sounded far too plausible but hardly mattered now. And neither did his request that she should move all her stuff out of the flat as he had another tenant lined up. She knew she must leave the flat but it meant she had nowhere to take Mum when she was discharged.

'To find my friend, Zillah Brown, there at the hospital too was surreal,' she said with a catch in her breath. 'They'd met by chance and it ended up like this,' she told Michael.

'The name's familiar,' he said. 'Doesn't Zillah Brown hold exhibitions at her studio in

23

Lyme? My eldest boy was doing some project on art at school and we went along. Huge affairs in acrylic, very colourful.'

'That sounds like Zillah,' said Kathryn. 'Always the flamboyant one. We go back a long way, Zillah and me. We did everything together until she left home for art school and I started teacher training. The other car was to blame, you know,' she added quietly. It was hard not to think ill of Zillah but how unfair was that?

Michael told Kathryn a little more of the set-up at the house as they drove the rest of the way to Bulbury Knap. His home was a cottage in the grounds. During the summer months he had two men working under him but there was no other help in the house than a housekeeper. The last one had let them down after only a few weeks.

'And now my mother will be doing the same,' said Kathryn sadly.

'Through no fault of her own,' Michael pointed out, drawing up at a road junction.

Kathryn was dreading telling the kind Hewsons that the housekeeper they thought they had acquired would no longer be able to look after them.

CHAPTER THREE

The house was in darkness. 'They keep early hours,' Michael said. 'There'll be a note. Some message. You've an overnight bag in the car?'

Kathryn nodded. Suddenly the place seemed unwelcoming and it was getting darker by the minute.

'Your car's all right here for now,' he said. 'But we'll drive round to the back. I've got a key.'

He waited for her to retrieve her bag and climb back into his vehicle. As they drove through an archway she could see that one downstairs light was on. This turned out to be the kitchen. Michael unlocked the door and ushered her inside.

The room looked bare and felt cold. Kathryn shivered. That she was not expected to return was obvious.

'Not to worry,' said Michael as if he could read her thoughts. 'They're a bit vague sometimes. I'm sure they'd want you to stay. Your mother's room will be ready. The best thing is for you to settle in there for the night. Come, I'll show you.'

Bemused, she followed him along the passage and up the wide staircase. He threw open a door at the end of another passage, flicked on a switch and stood to one side for

25

her to enter.

'In the morning things will seem better,' he said, stifling a yawn.

He withdrew so quickly there was no time to thank him. Kathryn yawned too, as she stumbled towards the bed. The central light dazzled the brass ornaments on the mantelpiece above the tiny Victorian fireplace and made her eyes ache. Almost blinded with fatigue she pulled off her jeans and jersey and collapsed beneath the covers of the soft bed.

A high-pitched sound entered Kathryn's dreams, intrusive and insistent. What was that? She sat upright in bed, her heart thumping as she glanced round the unfamiliar room. A fire alarm?

In seconds she was out, opening the thick curtains to let in the daylight and pulling on the clothes abandoned so hastily the night before.

She followed the noise down the stairs and along the passage to the open door of the kitchen. The acrid smell of burnt toast was overpowering and she rushed to throw the outside door and windows wide open. The smoke alarm subsided as the air cleared. She grabbed a cloth and removed the grill pan with its smouldering cargo, carried it outside and dumped it on the ground.

Phew! She wiped her hand across her forehead and then realised she was not alone. Sir Edwin Hewson, his stick tapping on the cobbles, was walking towards her. Lady Hewson, looking agitated, was close behind.

'Our apologies, Miss Marshall,' he said. 'It was remiss of us to leave the kitchen so hurriedly.'

'A strange cry,' Lady Hewson murmured. 'So many birds here but this was different. We wanted to identify it.' She looked sadly down at the incinerated toast. 'And now the toast is ruined.'

'I'll see to breakfast for you,' Kathryn offered. 'It's the least I can do after having a bed for the night.'

Sir Edwin bowed slightly. 'It's a pleasure to have you stay, my dear. Naturally we wish to know how your poor mother is. Mrs Marshall is one of our employees. We feel responsible for her.'

'I don't think you understand,' Kathryn said gently. 'My mother will be out of action for at least six weeks if not more. There's no way she can work as your housekeeper now. I'm so sorry.'

Lady Hewson smiled sympathetically as she indicated the larder door. 'We were afraid of that, dear.'

Kathryn opened it and found a spacious area containing a fridge and a bread bin. The butter was in a blue dish on a marble shelf above and looked soft. By its side lay a pack of bacon and a bowl of eggs. Suddenly she felt ravenously hungry.

27

While the bacon was sizzling in the large frying pan and Kathryn was breaking eggs into a bowl, she filled them in on everything that had happened.

'This is delicious dear,' Lady Hewson said as they began to eat.

Kathryn was touched. 'I'm glad you enjoyed it,' she said as she began to wash the dishes. 'I did too. But now I must tidy up upstairs and then get back to the hospital. I'm so grateful for the accommodation.'

'You have somewhere else to stay tonight?'

'Well, no, not yet.'

'Then you are most welcome to stay here,' said Lady Hewson.

Sir Edwin got to his feet. 'Yes . . . yes, an excellent idea. But on one condition.'

Puzzled, Kathryn looked at him as he stood leaning on his walking stick. Sir Edwin's eyes twinkled. 'You must cook us another excellent breakfast tomorrow!' he said.

He looked so proud of his suggestion that Kathryn couldn't help laughing. 'Of course I will,' she said. 'I'd love to.'

The warmth of their invitation washed over Kathryn as she went upstairs to get ready for her drive to the hospital. Tonight's accommodation had been solved. Great! But, of course, there was still the bigger problem remaining. Where would her mother stay when she came out of hospital that was suitable for someone with a broken ankle?

In spite of her worries Kathryn enjoyed her drive through grassy-banked lanes dotted with bright celandines and paler yellow primroses. A faint mist was rising from the fields and the sky looked hazy in the distance. She had phoned Helen before leaving Bulbury Knap and she had said they would be up to visit as soon as they could, probably tomorrow.

Kathryn smiled as she entered the ward and saw Sarah seated on a chair at the side of her bed. 'You look so much better, Mum,' she said in wonder as she kissed her and found a chair.

'That's because I feel I'm back in the land of the living,' said Sarah. 'Zillah will be back here in a minute. She's going home today as soon as a lift can be arranged.'

'You'll miss Zillah,' Kathryn said.

'She's good company,' Sarah agreed. She looked at Kathryn searchingly. 'And how are you, my love?'

Kathryn hesitated. Taking a deep breath, she told her quickly about the split with Nick glossing over the details and glad it was accepted without question. She had to pause, even now, to steady her voice and unclench her hands in her lap before she went on to talk of the accommodation she planned to get near the hospital so she could visit every day.

Sarah leaned forward in her seat. 'But what about your teaching work, dear?'

Kathryn smiled. 'I'm going to put it on hold for the moment. I need to get right away, do something different. And this is it.'

Sarah patted her hand and Kathryn was glad to see her face light again as Zillah came into the ward.

'Am I missing something?' Zillah asked, her colourful smock swinging as she pulled out a chair and sank down on it.

Sarah's cheeks were a little flushed as she looked from one to the other. 'Kathryn's giving up her flat in London and is planning on staying in the area for a while,' she said.

'So, Kathryn, where's your mum going when they let her out?' Zillah's warm voice seemed to echo round the ward.

Kathryn looked at her in dismay. She had deliberately avoided that subject and Mum hadn't raised it herself.

'You could come to me, Sarah,' said Zillah, leaning forward in enthusiasm. 'I'd look after you, I promise.' She got up from her seat as if to prove she could, gave a twist of pain and then plumped down again. 'I'd love it. My studio flat's right on the harbour front and there's plenty to watch all day long.'

'Oh but Zillah . . .' Sarah began.

'If it wasn't for me you'd be OK,' said Zillah, her voice deep. 'Please let Sarah come to me, Kathryn.'

Kathryn felt sorry for her. Wouldn't she feel just the same in the same position as her friend, blaming herself even though the accident wasn't her fault? 'But Zillah, you've got to think of yourself. You've been in an accident. You're probably still in shock.'

'Rubbish,' said Zillah, her voice scathing.

Kathryn looked at her mother and saw that she was smiling.

'I could be in here for days yet,' Sarah said. 'Let's wait and see how you feel then, shall we?'

'Kathryn can come and see for herself,' Zillah said as if she hadn't spoken. 'Inspect the place and so on. Too bad I can't fit more than one extra in.'

'Hold on,' Kathryn said, laughing. 'But thanks, Zillah. I'll be there as soon as I can.'

* * *

'Me?' Kathryn swung round from the sink and gazed at Sir Edwin in surprise. 'You wish me to take Mum's place as housekeeper here at Bulbury Knap?'

'In a temporary position, of course,' Sir Edwin said gruffly. 'Until your mother is fully recovered and able to take up her position.'

'But I've never done anything like that before,' she said, as she wrung out the dishcloth and pulled the plug out of the sink.

'If you could find it in your heart to help out an elderly couple we should be so grateful,' said Lady Hewson tentatively. She got to her feet and stood leaning her frail weight on the back of her chair.

31

'Indeed, my dear,' said Sir Edwin.

Kathryn hesitated. This amazing suggestion would mean that Mum's dream of working and living at Bulbury Knap hadn't come to an end after all. But . . . herself as acting housekeeper? She glanced around the kitchen. Surely she could prepare and cook meals for them easily enough and do the shopping and the cleaning? 'But isn't there anyone else you should talk to about this before offering the job to me?' she said.

A shadow flickered across Lady Hewson's face. 'Jane, our daughter, lives in New Zealand,' she said. 'Andrew looks after our interests when he's here. Such a dear boy. We're expecting Andrew any day now,' she added, smiling a little.

Kathryn glanced across at the photo on the dresser she knew was of Sir Edwin's great nephew. He looked serious, his dark hair smoothed flat. Mum would be so pleased her position would still be here for her when she was well again.

'I haven't any other plans at the moment,' Kathryn said, considering. Life here would be so different from Wimbledon, she thought, struggling to ban from her mind the painful vision of Nick and Anna together. 'You would need references,' she added. 'I'd be able to sort that out for you.'

'We mustn't rush you, dear,' Lady Hewson said. 'Talk it over with your mother when you see her today and let us know what you decide. You'll have time to see over the house first so you can see what would be expected of you?'

'Of course.'

*   *   *

The route through the house was tortuous with so many steps up and down. Kathryn could see that although the furniture was old and beautifully preserved there was an air of neglect about the place. One or two rooms showed signs that someone had tried to make them look lived-in. Sir Edwin threw open a door at the end of a long passage upstairs and then stood aside for the others to precede him.

The bed was a small four-poster with faded cream hangings. A walnut chest of drawers and wardrobe stood against one wall and a writing desk and chair on the other with a door leading into a spacious en suite. Kathryn exclaimed in delight.

Lady Hewson glowed with pleasure. 'This is Andrew's room, and the room next door he uses as his study,' Lady Hewson said. 'His computer is in there and all sorts of things we don't understand. It's kept locked, of course.'

*   *   *

Kathryn leaned on the warm windowsill and gazed down from the open window of

Zillah's studio at the busy harbour scene below. Although late in the season the place seethed with activity. People in holiday gear meandered about eating ice creams. Squawking seagulls added to the din of boats' engines and the salty breeze fanned her hair.

She still felt euphoric from her mother's pleasure in Sir Edwin and Lady Hewson's kind plan and her acceptance of it when she got back from the hospital yesterday. Helen, too, had been delighted. But there was still the question of finding somewhere for Mum since Helen's and Dan's small cottage in Cornwall was overflowing now that Dan's brother was living with them.

'If only it was more suitable for her here, Zillah,' Kathryn said now, hearing the longing in her voice.

Her friend's chair creaked as she leaned back. 'So what's wrong with it?'

'Mum would never get up those narrow steps with her leg in plaster and the room she'd have is higher still, above this one.'

Zillah, in her flapping smock, gazed back at her with the light of battle in her eyes. 'Are you saying it can't be done?' she demanded as she jabbed a paint-smeared finger in Kathryn's direction.

'This place is ideal for an artist like you,' said Kathryn, rubbing her arms as she turned to face the over-crowded room. 'But for Mum I'm afraid it's out of the question.'

                    *   *   *

The dread in Kathryn's heart deepened as
familiar landmarks began to appear on her
drive up the M3 towards London.

Even the flat key in the pocket of her best
jeans felt heavier than it should now she was
getting near. They had made no contact, she
and Nick, but hopefully everything in the
apartment was how she had left it.

She felt a lump in her throat. How could he
have done this to her, allowing her to find out
about himself and Anna in that humiliating
way? But she mustn't think of him, wouldn't
think of him. Concentrate on the driving, she
told herself. She had left Bulbury Knap this
morning as the sun was rising still bemused by
Sir Edwin and Lady Hewson's amazing offer
on her return from Zillah's studio.

'Naturally your mother will come here to
convalesce,' Lady Hewson said in her gentle
voice.

'Here?' said Kathryn in surprise. The
torturous staircases and the many uneven steps
from one part of the house to the other made
it highly unsuitable for anyone on crutches.
But Sir Edwin had offered Michael's help in
getting the invalid established in her room
upstairs.

'And if you feel you could take the
temporary post as housekeeper that would be

delightful,' Lady Hewson had added.

'Of course I will,' Kathryn said though she still felt doubtful about how it would all work out.

Another downside was her having to return to London for one night in order to put her affairs in order and to collect all her belongings from the apartment. But it had to be done and she would phone Helen on her return.

Unlocking the door of the apartment and stepping inside was painful, but at last it was done and she shut the outside door behind her and posted the key through the letterbox with relief. Nothing of her now remained in the place that had been home to her all these months.

CHAPTER FOUR

To Kathryn's surprise there were three vehicles already parked there in the large cobbled yard at the back of the house, two of them police cars. Her mouth was dry as she walked round to the front door to ring the doorbell.

The heavy door opened by a woman police constable. 'Miss Marshall?' she asked. 'I'm PC Janet Strong. Lady Hewson's expecting you.'

With a pang of shock Kathryn stared at the

pictures ripped off the walls and the table smashed on the floor. She went into the den and saw Lady Hewson's pale face and anxious eyes. Here at least the room had been left alone.

Lady Hewson struggled to her feet. 'Oh my dear,' she said. 'What a welcome back for you.'

Kathryn took her cold limp hand in hers. 'Please sit down, Lady Hewson,' she said.

'We've almost finished now and then we can leave you in peace,' said PC Strong.

As the police left Sir Edwin joined them followed by Andrew Hewson who frowned as he took up his stance on the hearthrug. He was as handsome as his photograph but now his eyes weren't laughing. For a moment Kathryn felt a twinge of fear.

'It's plain they knew it would be worthwhile breaking in,' Andrew said, looking straight at Kathryn.

'Did the police say how they know that?' said Sir Edwin.

Andrew shrugged his broad shoulders. 'No need, was there? You say you didn't ask for references? Very unwise, Uncle, in the circumstances, don't you think?'

'What circumstances?' Sir Edwin asked sharply.

Kathryn felt a flush cover her face as she realised what Andrew was implying. She had checked with the three referees she had chosen and a list of their details was in her bag.

The laugh Andrew gave sounded hollow. 'Do I need to spell it out?'

'Yes, my boy, I think you do.' Sir Edwin moved his weight from one foot to the other.

'Well then, here goes. You invite a stranger into your home, show her round, no doubt making a point of showing her all your most valuable things. Isn't that true, Uncle?'

Sir Edwin bowed his head slightly in acceptance.

'It wouldn't take much to suss out the best ways of entering the place. Any fool would see you have no alarm system installed.'

'But Andrew, you can't mean Kathryn?' Lady Hewson said in bewilderment. 'Kathryn's not a stranger. She's Mrs Marshall's daughter.'

Andrew looked triumphant. 'Exactly. And how much did you know about her when she turned up here?'

Kathryn clutched the back of a chair for support. 'It's outrageous and totally untrue,' she cried. 'I have the details of three people who will vouch for me.' She struggled to open the clasp of her bag but her fingers felt clumsy.

'Too late.' Andrew's lip curled. 'The damage is done. In my view you should be out of here right now, Uncle. I'll book you into a hotel for the night, longer perhaps. What do you say?'

'We stay here,' said Sir Edwin with a touch of hauteur.

'Your daughter has me to act on her behalf,' Andrew said. 'If you stay at Bulbury Knap I must insist that you ask Miss Marshall to leave immediately.'

Sir Edwin's knuckles tightened on his stick. 'How dare you, Andrew?' he demanded. 'I won't have it, d'you hear? You won't darken these doors again until you apologise to the young lady.'

The silence that followed his words sent shivers down Kathryn's spine. Andrew flicked his dark hair back and strode to the door. 'You'll regret this,' he spat out.

Lady Hewson sat with bowed head and her hands clasped in her lap. Sir Edwin cleared his throat. 'I'm sorry, my dear,' he said.

Kathryn felt a rush of sympathy for them. 'It might be best for me to leave Bulbury Knap at once,' she said gently.

Sir Edwin cleared his throat. 'We need you here now more than ever.'

Lady Hewson struggled to sit upright in her chair. 'Andrew was shocked and worried for us, that's all,' she said.

'Thank you,' said Kathryn. She was pleased by their faith in her. She knew that her mother coming to Bulbury Knap to convalesce with the place in its present state was now totally out of the question. She drew in a painful breath.

'What's missing is of no matter,' said Sir Edwin. 'They're objects, that's all.'

39

He sounded so sincere that Kathryn was touched. But their nephew's false accusations were another matter. From the hard expression in Andrew Hewson's eyes Kathryn had no doubt that he believed that she had tipped someone off to break in.

She would have an important decision to make in the near future but first she must see to their immediate comfort and then set about clearing up the mess.

'I'll have a word with Michael,' Sir Edwin said as if he could read her thoughts.

* * *

Michael Carey heaved the study table back into position. 'That was heavy,' he said, breathing hard.

Kathryn looked up from replacing books in the bookcase. 'This room is fairly reasonable now,' she said as she struggled to her feet and brushed the dust from the knees of her jeans. Exhaustion was beginning to get to her too.

Kathryn had looked at the bedrooms in dismay, aware that they wouldn't be habitable for some time. A quick phone call to Helen was all she had time for, but her sister had to know that Zillah's invitation to Mum wasn't feasible either.

A tiny long-disused attic room would be hers for tonight and she had plans to help Michael carry two single beds down to the den for Sir Edwin and Lady Hewson as a temporary solution.

Now she followed Michael to the long room at the back on the ground floor where Sir Edwin's treasures had filled the glass-fronted cabinets and display cases. Not any more. Doors hung open and broken glass littered the floor.

'Something wrong?' Michael asked.

Kathryn turned to him and tried to smile, though it was difficult. 'Sir Edwin and Lady Hewson don't deserve this and I'm so sorry for them. And now there's my mother to worry about when she comes out of hospital.'

Michael looked at her without speaking for a moment. He had made no comment about the state of things here at Bulbury Knap, but she didn't doubt he felt the desecration as much as anyone. His eyebrows drew closer together as if he was taking his time to sum things up. 'There's something else bothering you too,' he said at last.

Kathryn shrugged, biting her lip. The knowledge of Andrew's outburst against her was beginning to get to her. 'I don't like being accused of something that's not my fault,' she said.

Michael looked startled for a moment. 'Andrew's been getting at you, I suppose,' he said. 'What's he been saying?'

'Something totally untrue,' she said. 'No way was I casing the joint for a gang of thieves.'

A smile flickered in Michael's eyes and his lips twitched. 'Is that really what he thinks?'

Kathryn nodded, in no mood for smiling. 'That's bad enough, isn't it?' To her horror her lips trembled and she was glad he didn't press her to say more though he must have wondered.

They worked silently in the other rooms downstairs. She had the feeling that Michael was slow to judge others and liked to make up his own mind after due deliberation. She found herself wondering how he came to be working here. It must be a lonely life.

*　　　*　　　*

'Andrew wants a word with you when he gets back,' Sir Edwin said when Kathryn tapped gently on the door and went into the den.

Her heart missed a beat. Striving not to let the panic show on her face, she nodded and smiled. At least she now knew that Mum would be going to Helen's to convalesce even though it meant kicking out Iain, her brother-in-law, who had been living with them.

'You haven't had proper time yet to unpack your belongings and get settled in,' Sir Edwin said. 'I trust you've located somewhere suitable to sleep tonight?'

'A small room, right at the top,' Kathryn said. 'D'you mind if I make another phone call to my friend, Zillah? And afterwards I'll check

42

the kitchen and see what can be done about a meal.'

Lady Hewson looked at her gratefully. 'That sounds very good, dear.'

Andrew came into the kitchen a little while later looking as fresh and confident as if he had the power to set right all ills with a flash of those dark eyes. 'I think I owe you an apology,' he said disarmingly.

Taken aback, Kathryn let out the breath she had been holding.

'I was out of order earlier it would seen.'

'Believe me I'd do nothing to hurt your aunt and uncle or Bulbury Knap,' said Kathryn.

He nodded. 'So they tell me.'

'You still don't believe me?'

He picked up a mug from the draining board, looked at it and put it down again. 'It seems I'll have to.'

'You either do or you don't,' Kathryn said sharply.

He looked at her and a smile lit up his face with sudden charm. 'OK, you win. I apologise most abjectly. Will that do?'

He looked for a moment as if he would sink to his knees. His transformation from the malicious man who had accused her earlier was amazing, but for the sake of Sir Edwin and Lady Hewson she must take this olive branch without a murmur.

She nodded. 'Thank you,' she said.

'Right then,' he said with a laugh in his

43

voice. 'I can see there's nothing else for it but to convince you. A table at the best restaurant in town for two. A peace offering?'

He held his handsome head on one side and looked so appealing she smiled in spite of herself. 'Your aunt and uncle are still in shock. I can't leave them at the moment,' she said.

'Wednesday evening then, seven o'clock,' he said easily. 'I'll pick you up here. Make their bedtime drinks early and they'll be fine.'

*   *   *

The view of sea and coastline from The Brookside Hotel was breathtaking. Kathryn paused on the path from the car park, entranced at the golden shimmer of setting sun across the smooth sea and the shadows darkening the headlands in the distance.

Andrew smiled down at her as he indicated the flight of steps that led to the entrance. 'Like it?'

'It's perfect,' she breathed. She felt more relaxed now that the problem of Mum's convalescence was solved. Dan and his brother were driving up from Cornwall tomorrow. Dan would take Mum back with him while Iain set off on his travels in this area, researching the Jurassic Coast for a book and articles he was writing, apparently happy to free up his room for the invalid. Kathryn left her jacket in the cloakroom and joined Andrew in the foyer.

Their table was in the window. Andrew, seated opposite, smiled at her. She marvelled at the ease with which he steered the conversation away from his aunt and uncle and Bulbury Knap and talked instead of his business interests in North Devon where apparently he owned a hotel chain.

As the meal progressed she found herself laughing at Andrew's descriptions of his exploits as a young boy when spending holidays at Bulbury Knap. She could see quite easily why Lady Hewson was so fond of her husband's great nephew. And now Andrew kept his eye on the elderly pair, obviously having their interests at heart.

'I gather Sir Edwin enjoys the gardening groups that visit Bulbury Knap,' she said as they finished their dessert and Andrew ordered coffee.

'Ah yes, the groups,' Andrew said as if there had been no interruption. 'Uncle talks of taking more now to make more cash. Yes, he enjoys them coming but I've seen him when they depart . . . completely shattered. Far too much for him. Aunt Dorothy too. They won't admit it, of course.' He leaned back in his chair and frowned at the cup and saucer in his hand. 'Bulbury Knap needs to be fitted with an efficient burglar alarm. I won't rest easy knowing how simple it would be for those intruders to return. They didn't get much. They could come back for more.'

Kathryn shivered.

'My aunt and uncle can't afford it, of course.'

'But if more groups came couldn't we help . . . Michael and me. Between us we could take them round, couldn't we? Michael . . .'

Andrew drained his cup and leaned forward to replace it in its saucer on the silver tray. 'The gardener?' He gave a hollow laugh. 'Not an option, I'm afraid.'

The cold tones of his voice surprised her and she was silenced. Mum had told her how much Andrew disliked the man whom Sir Edwin and Lady Hewson relied on so heavily. It was tactless of her to mention him.

As they left at last the moon began to rise above the horizon. Andrew drove her back to Bulbury Knap in silence but when they arrived he made no move to get out of his car, saying he had a long drive ahead of him. With a smile and a wave he left her to go into the house alone.

Kathryn rose early a day or two later, determined to get the oven switched on for the breakfast rolls in good time so that afterwards she could continue with some of the cleaning she hadn't had time for yesterday.

Michael had already promised to remove the two single beds from the study as they were no longer needed there. Today was special because at twelve o'clock a Somerset Gardening Club was booked in for a visit.

46

Yesterday when Sir Edwin mentioned this he had looked brighter than she had seen him for days. She hoped it wouldn't all be too much for him, as Andrew had implied it might during their dinner together at the Brookside Hotel.

She loved the early mornings when she felt as if the house were her own. Her preparations complete, Kathryn wandered out into the sunny yard. Plenty of time to take a look round and to learn something more of her surroundings.

She could see that the buildings on the other side must have once been stables. There were other doors further along with windows either side of them. Kathryn crossed the cobbles to look closer. Obviously these had once provided accommodation for some of the work people on the estate but now there was no longer the staff to need it. Except Michael, of course, and he lived in a cottage in the grounds.

She turned the handle on the first door. Inside was a small room with a staircase in one corner opening into another room, obviously the kitchen. Feeling daring, Kathryn ventured upstairs and found two rooms, one smaller than the other that contained a bath on feet, washbasin and toilet. Dust and cobwebs decorated both rooms and the windows were smeary but the floor seemed sound.

Thoughtfully she went outside again,

emerging into the sunshine with an idea already forming in her mind. Why not invest some money in modernising some of this unused accommodation and letting it out during the holiday season?

Later, Kathryn was at the front of the house as Andrew's red Ferrari drove up and stopped. He opened the door and sprang out. 'Hi there, Kathryn,' he called as she came close. 'What's doing?'

'We're expecting a coach to arrive soon,' she said.

He frowned. 'I saw Uncle Edwin doing sentry duty at the entrance.'

'I hope he hasn't long to wait in this cool breeze.'

He shrugged as he slammed his car door. 'More fool him. I told him, it's ridiculous pandering to these groups.'

'Look, Sir Edwin's on his way back now,' Kathryn said, relieved. 'I've had this wonderful idea, Andrew,' she added, unable to keep it to herself any longer. Quickly she told him the details, flushing slightly with enthusiasm as she pointed out how beneficial financially it could be.

'It's not on,' he said, raising his voice as if she were hard of hearing.

'Not much needs doing to the cottages to make them habitable again. I'd be here to help, and Michael . . .'

'Michael?' He almost spat the name and she

48

was disturbed at the malice in his voice.

'But . . .' she began.

'Out of the question, d'you hear?' Andrew shouted. 'I want no more of this.'

'Dear boy, what's wrong?' Sir Edwin said, reaching them at last. He looked worried. 'Your aunt . . . ?'

Andrew turned on Kathryn. 'Now see what you've done.'

There was the sound of an engine, the crunch of coach wheels on gravel as the vehicle turned in at the entrance and came towards them. Andrew's car prevented the driver drawing up near the entrance but it was near enough for the emerging passengers to hear the venom in Andrew's voice and to witness Sir Edwin's sudden collapse.

CHAPTER FIVE

Kathryn leapt towards the limp figure of Sir Edwin but before she could reach him someone gave a shout and came running. Sir Edwin was beginning to stir as Michael Carey reached his side. The coach driver was there, too, but Andrew seemed to have melted away.

Michael slid his arm round his employer for support. To Kathryn's relief Sir Edwin insisted on struggling to his feet.

'A chair,' said Michael.

There was one inside the front door. Kathryn fetched it quickly and then went back into the house. Lady Hewson looked up from her embroidery with a smile as Kathryn opened the door of the den. 'Our visitors have arrived?'

'Sir Edwin was there to meet them,' Kathryn said, forcing herself to speak calmly. 'He's sitting out there now. He's going to be all right, Lady Hewson, but he had a little fall.'

'Oh dear.' Lady Hewson stood up shakily. 'Then I must go to him. Don't look so woebegone, dear. He trips sometimes. He's getting older you know.'

'It's happened before?'

'Not for a little while but we've grown quite used to it.'

Surprised at Lady Hewson's calm reaction Kathryn accompanied her outside. Sir Edwin smiled as he saw them. Kathryn still felt shaky but, ashamed of her weakness, looked round for Michael.

Michael joined her. 'We can carry this off, the two of us, don't you agree?' he asked quietly. 'Can you cope with coffee now?'

The confident smile he gave her was the incentive she needed. 'Yes, of course.' With a glance at Sir Edwin's retreating back as he and Lady Hewson made their way indoors, Kathryn turned to the group. 'If you like to follow me,' she said, smiling. 'Coffee will be served immediately.'

Later, in the large kitchen, Kathryn had time to think of Andrew Hewson's angry rejection of her idea about the renovating of the cottages. True, she had mentioned it just as the coach was arriving but Andrew had dismissed it at once with angry words. Maybe he was the kind of person who didn't like interference in his or his relations' affairs and considered it no business of hers.

Deep in thought, she drummed her fingers on the edge of the table. She looked up, startled, as Michael approached. He shrugged himself out of his jacket and placed it on the back of a chair. 'How goes it?' he asked.

'Fine. I think everyone's finished coffee now,' she said. It felt good to have him here, part of the team the two of them made to keep things normal.

'No hurry,' said Michael, eyeing the plate of biscuits.

'Help yourself,' she said. 'Coffee?'

He picked up a cup and held it towards her to be filled from the large pot. As he took a sip he glanced, frowning, at the window. 'I hope the rain's going to hold off,' he said. 'I understand everyone's brought picnic lunches to eat at the tables in the grounds.'

'What shall we do if it doesn't?'

He glanced round the crowded kitchen. 'There's not much room in here.'

'The conservatory?' she said. 'I know it's a mess but I can work on it while you're on your

51

tour of the gardens.'

She was rewarded with a grateful smile. 'If you're sure.'

'No problem,' she said easily. 'I've prepared a tray for the Hewsons. I'll take it along now.'

'You'll need an extra cup,' he said.

'Andrew?'

'Dr Duncan.'

She looked surprised.

'Just called in as he was passing,' Michael said. 'Or so they believe. Andrew got on to him straight away, as he always does when something like this happens.'

'Andrew did?'

Michael nodded. 'Dr Duncan's a family friend of long standing and he likes to check up on things at Bulbury Knap. He'll arrange for any tests he thinks necessary, you can be sure of that. One day he's going to suggest stopping these coach parties as being too much for Sir Edwin.'

Kathryn paused as she picked up the tray. 'Andrew was shouting at me as the coach arrived,' she said. 'It might have been the shock of that.'

'Andrew was shouting at you?' Michael sounded so stern that one or two people glanced their way. 'So how could that have been your fault?'

'I'll tell you later,' Kathryn said hurriedly, escaping with the tray.

Dr Duncan was in the den with her

employers just as Michael had said. He was standing up and preparing to go when she went in. Seeing the tray he sat down again.

'Thank you, dear,' said Lady Hewson. 'So kind. Richard, you'll have coffee with us? This is Kathryn who is looking after us at the moment.'

Dr Duncan smiled warmly at her. 'Hello there, Kathryn,' he said.

Clearing the conservatory took longer than Kathryn anticipated. The rain was beating down on the glass roof by the time she had finished and puddles were beginning to form on the crazy paving slabs outside.

There were pegs in the passage that would be useful now and the drips from the jackets wouldn't hurt the stone floor. She had the kettle on for more hot drinks by the time Michael came in with the first group.

'The others won't be long,' he told her, pulling off his wet jacket. Rivulets of water streamed down his face and he pulled out a handkerchief and mopped it.

Kathryn took the jacket from him, glad that the first arrivals looked content in spite of the weather. But perhaps true gardeners took no heed of the rain, she thought, marvelling at their stoicism.

Once everyone had finished eating and had drunk the tea and coffee Kathryn provided there was a move on. Most of them hadn't completed the tour of the grounds and decided to ignore the weather and do so while they had the chance.

At last Michael came back from making sure everyone was aboard the coach when it was time for it to depart.

She washed the last of the coffee mugs and dried her hands on the towel. 'No sign of Andrew?' she asked.

Michael shook his head as he glanced at his watch. 'I have to be back home in twenty minutes for school coming out. Mrs Pearce, our child minder, is having the day off. The rain's stopped. Fancy a walk across to my place while you tell me why Andrew instigated a bit of a scene you told me about? I can offer you tea and biscuits with Tom and Neville.'

Kathryn hesitated.

'You deserve a rest,' he said, at once understanding her reaction. 'I happen to know Sir Edwin's resting at the moment. They'd hate to be thought slave drivers, you know.'

Michael's cottage was less than five minutes walk away and during that time Kathryn filled him in on what had caused Andrew's outburst when the coach arrived. Michael's brooding silence disturbed her.

She could see Michael's cottage now in its small front garden bright with tulips. The paved path to the low front door looked freshly swept. The door stood open.

'Ah, my boys are here already,' he said.

They came running to meet their father and

54

he scooped them up in a tight hug. As he released them the elder one looked at Kathryn, his blue eyes so like his father's.

'This is Tom,' Michael said, ruffling his son's fair hair.

'Hello, Tom,' Kathryn said.

'And I'm Neville,' said his brother. 'I'm nearly as big as him but I'm only six.'

'I very nearly thought you were twins,' Kathryn said, smiling at them both.

Tom gave a snort of laughter. 'No way. We're nowhere near alike. Our hair's different. Neville's is nearly black.'

'Let's get inside,' said Michael. 'Drinks and biscuits all round and then Kathryn and I have some talking to do.'

'So,' he said as soon as the boys had escaped to the other small front room to watch television. He walked ahead of her carrying the tea tray and with his elbow flicked on the light switch. The room, illuminated, looked cosy. Outside a small branch tapped against the windowpane. 'I can't see anything wrong with that idea of yours. It makes perfect sense to me now you've raised the subject.' He placed the tray on a small table he hooked into position with his foot.

'Andrew is dead against it,' Kathryn reminded him as she accepted a cup of tea.

Pouring his own, Michael looked as if he was giving the matter serious thought. 'I'll take a look for myself tomorrow,' he said.

'Do you think that the garden clubs are too much for Sir Edwin?' she asked.

'Not if he's sensible and allows me to take some of the strain. But Sir Edwin and Lady Hewson are so interested in people who come, so keen to see their appreciation. They enjoy it all so much.'

'I can see that,' Kathryn said.

'Andrew is always pushing for Sir Edwin and Lady Hewson to give the place up.'

'And move away from Bulbury Knap?' said Kathryn with feeling. 'They'd hate that.'

'They would indeed,' said Michael. 'Andrew feels responsible for them, of course. Where is he now, by the way?'

'He'll have gone by now, I expect,' said Kathryn, hoping it was true. So much had happened already today she couldn't face more recriminations. 'He only came for the day and didn't want an evening meal.'

An outburst of shouting came from the other room. Michael got up to investigate and Kathryn glanced about her. The big round table pushed to the wall to give room for the three easy chairs was so highly polished it gleamed. Between two shining copper pots on the mantelpiece were several photographs of the boys at various stages in their young lives. Kathryn got up to take a closer look and saw that another photograph, slightly behind the others, was of a younger Michael with a young girl whose lively expression was so like

Neville's mischievous one that she smiled to see it.

'The boys' mother,' Michael said, returning.

Kathryn jumped, feeling awkward as she sat down again.

Michael cleared his throat as he seated himself too. 'She died giving birth to Neville.'

His tone was so final that she could only murmur something inadequate half beneath her breath. She knew instinctively that it would be an intrusion to offer sympathy and he wouldn't welcome it. She wondered if he had been living here at the time in this lonely cottage when he was left with two small sons.

Michael seemed to shrug off any sad feelings. His smile was warm as he talked some more of the empty cottages that used to house employees in the old days and had long been empty and disused. 'There's no reason that they couldn't be used again,' he said. 'It wouldn't take a big outlay to fit them up into holiday accommodation. It would be change of use, of course, but I can't see the planners objecting.'

'There's so much to do, so much to think about,' Kathryn said. Then, in case he thought she was complaining she added, 'I love the quietness and the beauty of it all here at Bulbury Knap.'

He looked very quietly pleased. 'You do?'

'My mother will love it too, when she comes.'

'How is she?'

'Enjoying being with Helen, my sister, down in Cornwall. She's glad to be able to keep an eye on things and not let Helen do too much now she's expecting another baby.'

'So it's working out well all round?' he said with satisfaction.

'Perfectly,' said Kathryn, feeling her eyes cloud at the sudden thought of Nick and the reason it was so convenient for her to be here. She hadn't thought of Nick all morning, not until now in fact and it was the middle of the afternoon. 'I'd better get back,' she added, standing up.

Michael stood up too. 'I'll walk you back. The boys will be all right for a little while.'

The distance seemed shorter to her now the route was familiar. In no time they had reached the gate to the pathway through the trees and were walking across the grass to the drive at the front of the house.

Someone, in jeans and a green sweatshirt with a rucksack on his back, was standing looking up at the front of the building.

Michael stopped abruptly. 'A visitor,' he said. 'Or has someone lost his way?'

Iain, of course! Helen had warned her that he might show up at Bulbury Knap in due course and now he was here. Kathryn rushed forward to greet him, delighted he had taken the trouble to seek her out.

'Iain!' she cried.

He caught her to him in a warm hug and then let her go again. She looked round for Michael but he had gone. 'Thanks for moving out to allow room for Mum,' she said.

The smile Iain gave her made him look years younger than his thirty years. 'It gave me the incentive I needed to take to the open road with an objective in mind,' he said cheerfully.

Even though he had often changed direction in his life and seemed content at the nomadic life he'd willingly embraced for her mother's sake Kathryn was grateful to him for making it sound so easy and uncomplicated. This project of Iain's was only last in a succession of job choices and sounded the best yet. She wondered if he'd started writing his book.

'And now I'll be able to report that all is well here,' Iain said. 'I take it that's so?'

Kathryn hesitated. He looked at her keenly. 'Uncle Iain's a dab hand at solving problems.'

'I don't think you'll be able to crack this one.'

'Just try me.'

They went through the arch and into the yard.

'Mmm,' said Iain, looking at Andrew's low-slung sports car with appreciation. 'A friend of yours?'

Kathryn shuddered. 'Not after the scene he created this morning.'

'Want to tell me about it?'

'Come inside, Iain, and bring that great rucksack with you.'

Iain was a good listener. As they drank their coffee at the kitchen table, Kathryn confided everything and found a great feeling of release in doing so to someone so closely connected to her family. Unlike Michael, who was an employee at Bulbury Knap, Iain could be truly objective.

'I don't understand it,' Iain said pensively when she had finished. 'It's as if the chap's deliberately blocking everything.'

'Michael has already suggested to him that he could organise a plant stall for the visitors,' she said. 'He thought it would be a good money spinner.

Iain raised an eyebrow. 'And?'

'Andrew wouldn't hear of it. Squashed the idea at once.'

'Doesn't anything occur to you in all this?' Iain asked. He sounded really serious.

'What do you mean?'

'Has Andrew Hewson done anything about the break-in?'

'How do you mean?'

'Been on to the police again? Got someone in to check the existing burglar alarm? Discovered how they immobilised it?'

Kathryn hesitated. 'He knows it's inadequate and that the Hewsons can't afford a better one.'

'So why not look into ways of raising the

money then? You'd think it the obvious thing to do in the circumstances.'

She was silent. When she'd been busy clearing out the conservatory earlier she had even considered raising the matter with Sir Edwin, but not wanting to jeopardise Mum's position, felt he might consider what she had to say completely out of order.

'We mustn't forget that Andrew was on to the doctor at once when Sir Edwin collapsed,' she said. 'And he comes so often to see them.' She glanced surreptitiously at her watch.

Iain drained the last dregs of coffee from his mug. 'I must be off.' He got to his feet and hauled up his rucksack.

She heard Andrew's car start up and the roar as he set off through the archway far faster than was safe. 'You're not going already?' She tried to keep the relief from her voice that the two men hadn't met. Not this time, anyway.

As he reached the outside door Iain paused to fish in the back pocket of his jeans and pulled out a card. 'This is my mobile number. Give me a buzz when you get some time off.'

He shot her an unfathomable look. 'I'll go now and leave you time to think about it. Have a word with your employers about your idea, why don't you? Talk it through. Sounds as if the chap, Michael, will back you up. I don't suppose for one moment that Andrew discussed it with anyone. He sounds a mite high-handed to me.'

Kathryn smiled wryly. 'There's no way I can take anything upon myself without falling foul of Andrew.'

'Coward!'

CHAPTER SIX

Kathryn stood looking out at the yard through the smeary cottage window, imagining clean paint on the walls and flowery curtains blowing in the breeze. When serving breakfast this morning her employers had been concerned that she should have some time to herself and on impulse she had asked for permission to take a look inside the empty cottages across the yard.

Sir Edwin had helped himself to toast. 'The workmen's cottages? Of course, my dear. They're structurally quite safe so you'll come to no harm.'

'The workers on the estate lived there long ago,' Lady Hewson said.

Sir Edwin gave a small sigh. 'No-one would want to live there nowadays.

'No electricity . . .'

'There was water laid on,' Lady Hewson said. 'They managed quite well. But first, dear, we have something to show you.'

Sir Edwin pulled a folded sheet of paper

from his pocket and handed it to Kathryn.

'Andrew printed out Jane's e-mail for us,' Lady Hewson said proudly.

Kathryn saw that the words on the subject line of the e-mail were *Crisis at Bulbury Knap*. In dismay she read that Jane was deeply concerned about the state of the house and of her parents' ill health and inability to cope. She wanted them to move out immediately while Andrew dealt with what had to be done. A wave of anger at the absent Jane swept over Kathryn so quickly she gasped.

'So worried about us, dear Jane,' said Lady Hewson calmly. 'There's really no need for her to come all the way from New Zealand and we shall tell her so when we speak to her on the telephone.'

'Your daughter's planning to come over?' asked Kathryn.

'It would be lovely to see her, of course,' Lady Hewson said wistfully.

But not if the object of the visit was to turf them out of their beloved home and put it on the market, Kathryn thought as she turned away from the window and went downstairs. She dusted down the front of her jeans as she shut the front door behind her.

'Kathryn!'

She spun round. 'Andrew.'

'You're wanted indoors,' he said. 'There's been a phone call. Urgent, my uncle said. You'd better hurry.'

Kathryn hadn't known what to expect as she rushed indoors. Now, a couple of hours later, on the drive to Cornwall with Iain seated in the car beside her, she wondered at her calmness on hearing that her mother had been taken to hospital again after a fall in the road outside the Polmerrick cottage.

The Hewsons had said at once that she could take the rest of the day off, that Andrew was here and would stay overnight so Kathryn was not to worry about hurrying back. Iain's chance phone call soon after was welcome and so was his offer to accompany her on the long drive.

She was grateful for Iain's continuous talk about the Jurassic Coast. He had begun investigating the Devon end, the oldest section, and was already planning his book. The cliffs on their own part of the coast were made up from rocks that dated from the Lower Jurassic period of approximately 180 to 200 million years old capped by rocks from the Cretaceous Age of about one hundred million years old.

'I see,' Kathryn murmured though of course she didn't. The numbers meant nothing to her in her present state of mind. They arrived in the crowded hospital car park just as someone was pulling out of a space in the corner.

'Back to square one, I'm afraid,' Helen said when she saw them, her voice clipped.

'How bad is she?' said Kathryn. 'What

happened? Is it worse than you thought?'

'She insisted on going out for a walk by herself and fell off the kerb on the other side of the road. Only a few steps from the house. I didn't know at first. She collapsed you see. Someone rang the door bell. You'll say it's all my fault.'

'Hey, calm down,' Iain said. 'No-one's blaming you.'

'I wanted Mum to come to me,' said Helen, close to tears. 'I wanted to look after her.'

Kathryn started to say something but was silenced by a warning glance from Iain. Maybe it was too much for Helen having Mum with her at this time, she thought as they walked to the ward. If so something would have to be done to ease the situation. But what?

Fortunately the damage to her mother's ankle wasn't as bad as expected though it would set her back a few weeks. Things could be a lot worse.

They ate a quick meal in a service station near the start of the M5 at Exeter.

'Zillah phoned last night wanting to know how Mum was,' Kathryn said as they set off again. 'You've heard me speak of Zillah, best friend . . . the artist down in Lyme?'

'The cause of all your mum's troubles?'

'It wasn't Zillah's fault,' Kathryn said, feeling herself flush.

'I know, I know. Calm down.' There was amusement in Iain's voice now.

'Sorry.' She had been too quick to rise and felt the tension drain out of her as she laughed with him.

'How's she coping since the accident?'

'The insurance money isn't enough to replace her old banger, but she's got a big commission on and experts to be paid up front so she's going to be doing something positive about that.'

'Great. She sounds quite a girl,' said Iain.

They were nearing Lyme now, beginning to descend the steep hill to the harbour with the vision of the sea and the coastline ahead of them stretching into the distance.

'There's billowing smoke down there,' Iain said, craning forward to look. 'Right by the harbour by the look of it.'

'Zillah's studio! That's where it is.'

Iain released his seat belt and half stood to get a better look. 'Can't quite see,' he said, subsiding again and clicking the belt in position. 'There's more smoke now. Masses of it.'

The road ahead was blocked but the entrance to the car park on the right was clear. She drove in and parked. 'I'll have to check on Zillah,' she said urgently. You don't have to come, Iain. You could walk to your place from here.'

He sprang out, shrugging on his jacket as he elbowed the door shut. 'Of course I'm coming.'

They hurried towards the side exit that led

66

down to the Cobb. A fire engine, its siren blazing, was negotiating the cobbles in order to reach the building on the far side of the harbour that housed Zillah's studio. Another burst of smoke rose in the air.

'Smoke but no flames yet,' Iain pointed out. 'Come on, let's get round there.'

A lick of flame rose in the air.

'Let me pass, let me through,' Someone shouted from behind. Kathryn spun round. 'Zillah!' she cried in relief.

Her friend, with staring eyes and hair awry, pushed her away unseeingly towards them.

'Stand back, please. It's not safe to pass,' someone called out.

'It's my place on fire,' she screamed. 'You've got to let me through.'

Instantly Iain grabbed Zillah's arm to prevent her going farther. 'Do as they say. It could be dangerous.'

She tried to shrug him off. 'Let me go!'

'Zillah,' cried Kathryn again.

'Kathryn?' Zillah sobbed.

'It's me,' said Kathryn, holding on to her too. 'Iain's with me. Stay here with us, Zillah, until it's safe. Let them deal with it. Please, Zillah.'

'I went out,' Zillah moaned. 'I didn't know. What are they doing?' She rubbed her arm across her eyes. She struggled free and stood upright. Her purple and orange jacket swung open to reveal a paint-smeared smock beneath.

Somehow, seeing that, a lump rose in Kathryn's throat. Zillah, for all her apparent strength, was deeply vulnerable.

'The flames have gone now,' someone shouted.

Kathryn gazed across that harbour at the building. The black pall that had hung over it earlier had subsided a little too.

Beside her, Zillah gasped. 'What happened? Oh, what happened? I wasn't out long. When will they let me back?'

Much later, seated in the café, from where they could see flickering lights across the harbour, Kathryn leaned back in her seat feeling exhaustion seep through her until her limbs seemed weightless. The likely outcome of the fire seemed horrendous.

Iain yawned. 'We've had a long day,' he said. 'My landlady here has rooms vacant. Why not book in there for tonight, Zillah?'

Zillah nodded. 'I've been selfish, haven't I, keeping you here?'

'I'll come back with you to your studio tomorrow, Zillah,' Iain offered.

Kathryn smiled at him. No-one would think he and Zillah had only just met. But Iain was like that, friendly and willing to help anyone in a worse situation than himself. When Zillah had refused to leave the scene he had waited with her gladly.

At last Zillah began to realise that she

wouldn't be able to do anything more until the morning. With a last look across the dark water, she allowed herself to be led to the car and then to the house where Iain was staying.

*   *   *

Iain phoned next morning as Kathryn was clearing away the breakfast things. 'Zillah's been allowed back in to view the damage,' he said. 'What a mess. The smell's horrific.'

'Are all her paintings damaged?' Kathryn asked, concerned. 'Is it really bad?'

'They're in a poor state. Most destroyed completely. A few things not touched. The smoke's stained some of the blank canvasses but others are all right. Some of her paints are OK too, I think.'

Kathryn sighed, imagining the scene. Not good then, as she had expected. 'What are you doing now?'

'Getting stuff out that can be salvaged. The landlord's here now and some of the other tenants. The place'll be boarded up for the time being.'

A plan had been forming in Kathryn's mind as they were speaking but she couldn't voice it until she had spoken to Sir Edwin. Plenty of space in the derelict cottages across the yard to store any amount of painting equipment.

She found Sir Edwin in the long sitting-room leaning on his stick as he gazed round

69

the empty space. He gave a start as she came in. 'You need me, my dear?'

'I've a favour to ask, Sir Edwin,' she said.

Hesitantly she told him of her idea of helping Zillah out of a tight spot. He agreed immediately as she knew he would. She hesitated for a moment as she turned to leave. Should she mention Andrew's dislike of the cottages being used? But no. Andrew had objected to them being let out for living in. This was merely for the storage of property on a temporary basis. Surely he couldn't object to that?

*   *   *

Kathryn propped open the cottage door and set to work. Sweeping was no problem or gathering up the dust but without electricity there was no way of putting a heater in here as Lady Hewson wished.

She looked up, startled, as a shadow fell across the open doorway. Michael, his arms full of grey army blankets, stepped inside.

'Don't look so bemused,' he said with a smile. 'We keep these stored in the old stable at the back of my place in case of emergency. According to Sir Edward that time has come.'

'And you brought them over here specially?'

'My vehicle's outside.'

Kathryn had been so absorbed in her work that she hadn't heard it.

'I'll dump them over here where you've swept, shall I?' Michael said. 'Lady Hewson thought they'd be suitable to spread out on the floor so your friend's belongings won't get dusty.'

'They'll make a fine carpet,' she said.

He grinned. 'Making plans to furnish the place?'

'How did you guess?' Being here with Michael felt companionable because he understood and approved her ideas.

Together they covered half the floor area with the blankets. 'Hiding the bare boards makes all the difference to the place,' he said.

'Almost as if it was going to be lived in,' she agreed.

'Andrew will think the same if he sees it like this,' said Michael.

She smiled, liking the feeling they were in this together. 'Zillah's stuff will be stored here temporarily. That's all.'

'How soon will she move it here?'

'She can't get a van and driver until this evening. But I thought I'd need to prepare the place as soon as I could so it's all ready for her.'

'She's got a friend in you, Kathryn,' Michael said.

She felt herself flush at the expression in his eyes. 'Sir Edwin and Lady Hewson are so kind.'

He shrugged, smiling. 'It's good to see this

71

place being made use of. Let me know if you need any help in unloading. The quicker it's done the better.'

She nodded. 'Thanks.'

'Finished over here for the moment?'

'All done,' she said in satisfaction.

Outside in the yard with the early sunlight on her face, Kathryn took a deep breath of pure pleasure. She was glad that through her Zillah had somewhere to store her property while she got her studio sorted out. It would be safe enough here.

The van rattled into the yard as Kathryn was washing up at the sink. She wiped her hands and rushed out to greet it.

The driver's door opened and he leapt out, gazing round him with a bemused expression on his young face. 'This it?'

Zillah had more difficulty extricating herself. Her smock caught on the hinge as she tried to jump down. She pulled it loose with a ripping sound and gave a snort of impatience. 'This is Bob,' she said. 'No room for Iain. He was miffed, I can tell you.' Her hearty laugh rang out across the courtyard.

'One moment and I'll get some extra help organised,' Kathryn said. A quick phone call and Michael would be here.

'Where d'you want it put, Kathryn?' Zillah nodded at the open door of the cottage. 'In here? This is a great place. You've done me proud.'

'We aim to please,' said Kathryn, smiling.

The van drove off at last, Zillah leaning out of the passenger window and waving enthusiastically. She seemed to take something with her out of the turbulent atmosphere that had consumed the place while the two men man-handled the larger pieces inside the cottage.

Now, in the sudden calm, Kathryn turned to thank Michael.

He was smiling as he wiped one hand down the side of his jeans. 'Quite a character, your friend,' he said.

Kathryn nodded. He sounded approving and she was glad of that. Not everyone could cope with Zillah's exuberant personality.

He glanced across at the cottage. 'All locked up?'

'Is there a key?'

He frowned. 'Sir Edwin's not mentioned one?'

'No, never.'

'Then there probably isn't one. It's too late now to do anything about it but I'll get into town for a new lock and key first thing. Should be OK anyway for tonight.'

Kathryn nodded. 'Thanks.' Andrew had left Bulbury Knap and certainly wouldn't be back before morning.

*   *   *

Kathryn shivered at the chilliness in the air as she came down to the kitchen the following morning. The stone flooring in the passage made it seem colder than it was.

To her surprise she heard voices. Sir Edwin and Zillah were seated at the kitchen table drinking tea. The electric kettle was steaming quietly to itself and on the draining board the brown liquid from a couple of tea bags oozed around them in a gluggy mess. Something was wrong here surely? She had seen Zillah off in the van late yesterday evening on its return journey to Lyme. Her smock was a clean one today and she had combed her hair.

'What are you doing here, Zillah?' Kathryn switched the kettle off and then put the tea bags into the pedal bin and wiped the draining board clean. Zillah really was the limit. She couldn't have got here this early from Lyme so she must have returned late last night and stayed somewhere on the estate. No prizes for guessing where.

'This tea is excellent,' Sir Edward said. 'How glad I am I rose early and discovered you out in the yard, my dear. I trust you had a good night?'

Zillah let out a relieved-sounding sigh. 'I slept like the dead,' she said.

'But where exactly?' asked Kathryn.

'Sit down, Kathryn,' Zillah invited, waving her hand at a vacant chair as if she were the hostess here. 'It's OK, honestly. This kind man

74

invited me to stay when I returned by taxi late last night.'

'You woke Sir Edwin?'

'I came downstairs in search of a drink of water,' Sir Edwin said gently.

Kathryn was silent, imagining the scene . . . Sir Edwin in this thick dressing gown unbolting the back door on hearing a vehicle draw up outside with not a thought of the break-in that had occurred so recently or of any danger he might be in.

'I couldn't bear to be apart from my things a moment longer, not after what they'd been through,' said Zillah with a shudder.

'Quite right, my dear,' Sir Edward said approvingly.

Kathryn looked at him questioningly. 'You mean you don't mind Zillah staying in the cottage until her studio is sorted out, Sir Edwin?'

'I think it's a splendid idea. I shall get Michael on to it immediately. We'll need to get some furniture down from the attics to make the place habitable.'

'I'll pay rent,' Zillah said, running her hands through her hair and turning it into an unkempt mess.

Zillah still looked shocked, Kathryn thought. But that was nothing to what poor Andrew would look when he found out that one of the cottages was to be occupied against his wishes. Her idea of turning the cottages into a moneymaking proposition for the Hewsons seemed to be coming to pass without any help from her.

Smiling, Kathryn glanced at the clock. 'Lady Hewson will be down soon,' she said. 'I must make a start on breakfast.'

Zillah sprang up, knocking a teaspoon to the floor with the edge of her bright smock. She bent down to scrabble for it. 'Let me help,' she said, her voice muffled.

The telephone rang as Sir Edwin was finishing a second breakfast with Lady Hewson.

'Andrew wishes to speak to you,' Kathryn said as she returned to the kitchen from answering it. The insurance quote had come through and Andrew, on the phone from Harrogate where he was about to attend a conference, wished to pass on the good news. What he was likely to hear in exchange from his uncle about Zillah's presence here at Bulbury Knap might well ruin the day for him.

When Sir Edward came back Kathryn could see that all was not well.

'Andrew is changing his plans and will be here tomorrow instead of next week,' Sir Edwin said as he sat down heavily. His stick slid to the ground. He said no more but his expression was anxious as he finished his meal.

CHAPTER SEVEN

Later, as dusk turned to night, Kathryn slipped out of a side door of the house and walked across the drive. She had worked hard all day, helping Zillah settle in to the cottage. Michael had not only done as Sir Edwin asked and found suitable pieces of furniture from the attics but he had also found time to purchase a new lock and fix it to the cottage door.

Once in place the old rather dusty table and chairs, chest of drawers and the narrow single bed looked as if they had always been there. Kathryn had done a good job on sprucing them up and Zillah was delighted.

She was also pleased with the box of goodies Lady Hewson had thoughtfully sent across to keep her going until she could shop for herself and also with some spare kitchen utensils Kathryn had found for her.

Zillah's exuberance was beginning to return now that she had somewhere of her own to work while she awaited the outcome of the fire to her studio. Kathryn was pleased, too. Now she craved a breath of pure air before falling into bed.

There was much to think about because events had moved fast. And one of these was worry about Andrew's likely reaction. He had always been against any suggestion that the cottages could be a viable way of raising money for the estate so why should he change his opinion now? Seeing Zillah in occupation, although only temporarily, wouldn't exactly fill him with delight.

Sighing, she moved aside a branch from a weeping willow to reach the path to the lake. The moonlight on the water was magical.

The figure, standing motionless on the other side might have startled her if she hadn't known at once that it was Michael. His tall frame was leaning against the solid trunk of an oak tree. She gazed across at him, thinking he hadn't seen her. Somehow the light on the water and the scented dusk seemed a fitting background for the person who shared her deep concerns about the place and who understood exactly how things were.

Oh yes, he had seen her. He raised his hand in greeting and called across the water to her in his deep voice. 'Hi there, Kathryn. I thought you were a wood nymph appearing so suddenly.'

She watched as he walked round to join her, bending low every now and again to avoid overhanging branches. In the distance a dog barked.

'I needed to come out,' she said breathlessly. 'It's so beautiful here. I had to think.'

He regarded her in silence for a moment. 'When does he come?' he asked at last.

'He's in Harrogate,' she said. 'He'll leave tomorrow morning, as soon as he can.'

'Early evening then?'

She nodded, imagining Andrew's arrival. She saw him drive into the yard, ram on the handbrake as he caught sight of the open door of the cottage with Zillah leaning against the door frame so obviously at home. 'There's bound to be a fuss,' she said.

She was aware of a slight movement from Michael and knew that he frowned. 'Sir Edwin will stand firm about your friend,' he said. 'He's stronger than you think.'

'Mentally perhaps,' she agreed. 'But not physically. And Andrew in a temper is not a pretty sight.'

Michael gave a deep-throated laugh and to her surprise she found herself joining in. 'It's not funny,' she gasped.

'There's nothing we can do about it, you and I,' he pointed out, the amusement still in his voice. 'Except prevent them coming face to face until the first flush of anger is past. And we're not even sure that it will come to that.'

This was more than Kathryn dared hope even though Michael sounded almost as if he believed it. 'I'll explain the situation to Zillah first thing tomorrow and ask her to lie low,' she said. In normal circumstances her friend would relish a fight. No way would Zillah skulk away indoors hiding from anyone. But, more subdued because of what had happened to her studio, she might just listen to her. It was worth a try.

'There's not much that Andrew can do, you know,' Michael said. He seemed to hesitate for a moment as if he wished to say more. The silence was disturbing.

'He can make life very uncomfortable for his uncle and aunt,' she murmured, conscious of the man at her side as she had never been before.

'As long as he doesn't try to stop the next Garden Club visit,' Michael said.

'Three days' time,' she murmured. 'Sir Edwin is buoyed up about it already.'

'A club from Somerset,' Michael said. 'They come every year.'

There was nothing more to be said about it really. They would have to wait and see what happened. She raised her face, aware of the silence around them and trying to gain some comfort from it.

Michael took a step towards her and then she was in his arms, his lips pressing so hard on hers she could hardly breathe.

For a stunning moment she relaxed against him. Then, realising what was happening she broke free with a gasp. 'No, no, please. I can't . . . ' She saw Nick's face in front of her, saw his features harden. Thinking of him had broken the moment.

She looked at her hands and found they were trembling.

Michael was her friend, her confidante, the only person here at Bulbury Knap who understood how important it was to her to make things possible for her mother to take up her place here. She cared for Sir Edwin and Lady Hewson as she knew he did. He was like a loving older brother. Or so she had thought.

Ashamed of her reaction, she turned away and wiped her hand across her face. 'I'm sorry,' she murmured.

They began to walk alongside the lake, their feet rustling in the fallen leaves on the path. The moon had gone behind some clouds now and a chill wind blew. She shivered.

'You're cold,' he said. 'I'll walk you back to the house.'

She could think of nothing more to say and was grateful that he seemed to understand her need for silence. As he bid her goodnight his voice sounded as it always had, deep and reassuring. She hurried upstairs to bed thinking that she must have dreamt the feel of Michael's lips pressing down hard on hers. But in her heart she knew she hadn't.

*　　　*　　　*

Kathryn finished polishing the bureau in the den the following afternoon and then checked her watch. Her employers were lunching late today and she was making the most of the extra time to give the room a good clean before they needed to use it. She had resisted the temptation to check on Zillah after seeing her this morning setting up her easel in the yard and laying out her paints on a box by her side.

'What a great place to work,' Zillah had said, waving her arms about in her enthusiasm. 'Plenty of space, you see. I've got a big commission I haven't started yet. Abstracts, large ones.'

Kathryn was pleased that she felt settled enough to start work straight away but suppose Andrew arrived early and found her working there? Zillah had promised, though, that later she would make herself scarce so that she'd be out of the way when he came.

She spent the afternoon discussing the menus for the following week with Lady Hewson and then driving her to the committee meeting of the Ladies' Guild in the next village. On her return the sound of young voices coming from the yard alerted her to the fact that school was out and Michael's sons had discovered Zillah at work at her easel.

She heard her loud laugh and went to investigate. Obviously enjoying herself, her friend was splashing colour on the canvas in front of her, watched intently by Tom and Neville. It was a happy scene in the sunshine, the faces of the two young boys alight with enthusiasm. Tom, tall for his age and so like his father, stood slightly behind his brother.

'Hi there, Kathryn,' Zillah called.

'I want to be a painter when I grow up,' Neville informed her as she approached. His dark hair was standing up in peaks as if he had kept running his hand through it and his freckles seemed to stand out on his face in his enthusiasm.

'I've said he can have a go soon,' said Zillah. She dipped her brush in a pile of cadmium red and dashed it on the canvas. 'This is how I'm feeling right this minute, itching to take on the whole world.'

'It looks like fire,' said Tom solemnly.

Zillah paused, her brush held in the air. Then she lay it down on her palette. 'You're right, Tom. Fire . . . yes, flames that are hot and cleansing and clearing all before them.'

Kathryn glanced at her watch. 'Andrew could be here at any time.'

'Will he mind you painting out here?' asked Tom.

Zillah grimaced and looked at Kathryn apologetically. 'I'll pack away.'

'It's not his yard,' said Neville.

'Listen,' said Tom. Lines furrowed his brow as he glanced towards the archway.

Kathryn paused. Definitely a car. The engine cut out. Thank goodness it wasn't coming through the archway to where they were. Dare she hope it was a visitor for the Hewsons or Lady Hewson being given a lift home from her meeting because it finished early?

'I'll pack up,' said Zillah, leaping to her feet and scattering tubes of acrylic paint in an untidy heap at her feet.

'No,' said Kathryn, surprising herself at her sudden feeling of calm determination. 'Why should you, Zillah? You're here at Sir Edwin's invitation. Stay right where you are.'

The four of them froze, listening. Except for a blackbird's warning call and some twittering in the trees behind the cottage no sound disturbed the cold air. Zillah let out a long breath. 'Phew,' she said. 'Fighting talk, Kathryn.'

'And why not?' Kathryn said with spirit. Too long had she been afraid of Andrew's reactions to anything that happened at Bulbury Knap. Instead of this jittery feeling she should be confident that Sir Edwin would deal with his nephew as he thought best.

Both boys scrabbled to pick up the scattered tubes of paint and then thrust them at Zillah who held out an empty box for them. As the tubes clattered into it Neville grinned at his brother. Tom gave him a look of such sternness that Zillah laughed. 'Peace before the storm,' she said. 'You two boys had better clear off home before anything happens.'

'Oh, no,' said Neville in disappointment.

'Come on,' said Tom, taking charge. 'We're supposed to be at home anyway.'

Kathryn brushed her loose hair away from her face, wondering what to do next . . . rush to see if any visitor needed welcoming or stay here to support Zillah? The sound of the arrival of a second vehicle made her mind up for her. 'I'll have to go, Zillah,' she said.

The car had stopped now, somewhere out of sight.

'Best of luck,' Zillah called after her. Kathryn walked through the archway to see if she was needed and found Lady Hewson being helped from a Honda Civic that had drawn alongside Andrew's red Ferrari.

'Ah there you are, dear,' her employer said when she saw Kathryn. 'I've been given a lift home. So kind.'

Kathryn smiled at the grey-haired woman in the driving seat. Lady Hewson waved as the car moved off and then turned to Kathryn. 'I see Andrew is already here,' she said with satisfaction. 'I'll just go and tidy up.'

Kathryn took her employer's heavy-looking bag from her and together they went indoors. A murmur of voices came from the den and Kathryn felt a stir of anxiety.

'I'll make tea and bring it through,' she said.

In the kitchen she started the preparations automatically, her mind on Zillah making herself at home in the cottage, helped by Michael's two boys. Tom and Neville seemed to have attached themselves to her in the short time her friend had been here. She wondered if Michael knew where they were.

She carried the tray through to the den, pushing the half-open door fully open with her shoulder. Andrew took the tray from her in silence and placed it on the table. He had removed the jacket of his dark suit and placed it on the back of a chair as if he had some Herculean task ahead and meant soon to get down to business. She glanced at Sir Edwin standing with his back to the window and saw that his expression was thoughtful.

'Perhaps you'd pour for us, Kathryn my dear,' Sir Edwin said.

'One minute,' said Andrew, looking hard at her. 'I believe you have a lot to do with this?'

Kathryn was not to be ruffled by his aggressive tone. 'With what?'

Sir Edwin cleared his throat. 'I have been telling Andrew about the unfortunate fire, my dear, and our offer to your friend to store her belongings in one of the old cottages.'

'And not only her belongings it seems.' Andrew threw back his dark head and glared at his uncle.

'And that is a problem for you?' Kathryn asked.

He gave her a look of such fierceness she took a step back.

'Of course not,' Sir Edwin said. 'The poor young lady needed somewhere to stay for the moment, Andrew, and I was glad to be able to provide it. No problem at all.'

Andrew hunched his shoulders. 'No problem you say? And you've accepted this person's offer to pay rent then, have you?'

'You don't think we should?' Sir Edwin looked anxious. 'Perhaps not, but the young lady insisted.'

Andrew gave a short laugh. 'I'll bet she did. She saw the chance to get a firm foothold here and took it.'

Lady Hewson broke the startled silence that followed. 'I don't think it's like that at all,' she said. 'She's Kathryn's friend you know, Andrew, not some stranger we know nothing about.'

'Kathryn's friend? And you don't think that's worrying?'

Sir Edwin ignored the insinuation behind the words. 'You're quite right about one thing, my boy. We must make a point of not accepting any money from her. She's our guest here at Bulbury Knap and as such should be treated as a friend of the family.'

'I shall be looking into the question of allowing her to remain on the estate,' Andrew said. 'And I shall certainly speak to your solicitor about the situation.'

Kathryn felt the keenness of Andrew's glance in her direction. She hadn't heard the last of this from him. For the time being, though, he said no more and accepted a cup of tea from her with a slight nod of thanks.

Kathryn glanced at the box of brilliant pink cyclamen Michael had placed at his feet on the cobbled yard as she emerged from the kitchen for a few minutes restorative air this bright February morning. She paused, surprised to see Michael so smartly dressed at this time of day.

'What gorgeous colours,' she said. 'Are they for the house?'

He nodded. 'Lady Hewson is fond of them. She wants the place to look welcoming for the Garden Club visit tomorrow. I thought I'd drop one off for Zillah at the same time to brighten up the cottage. I know she likes them.'

'You do?'

Michael gazed down at the flowers, a smile curving his lips. His white shirt gleamed in the sunshine and his jeans looked new.

'Zillah's in Lyme at the moment,' said Kathryn.

He looked disappointed. 'I'll leave it outside her door then.' He made to pick up the box again but then hesitated, as if suddenly remembering something. 'So, how's it going then, Kathryn? With Andrew, I mean?'

She sighed. 'I can take aggression and everything else. But not cold and polite. What's he playing at, Michael?'

He frowned. 'Some devious plan afoot, I

shouldn't wonder.'

They looked at each other in silence. Then his face softened. 'It's useless to worry, Kathryn. There's nothing we can do at the moment.'

'Except make the garden visit the success of the century.'

'That's the spirit.'

'He wants Zillah out of course.'

'And not only Zillah.'

'Me too?' She knew it was true, of course. By agreeing to stay on at Bulbury Knap to keep the position open for her mother she had helped make it possible for the Hewsons to remain here. 'So why doesn't he want Sir Edwin and Lady Hewson to stay on here if it's at all possible?'

'You're aware of what Andrew's business is?'

'Hotel management. I know he's got a string of places to look after.'

'Maybe he wants to strike out on his own.'

She looked at him, startled. 'He'd actually turf his aunt and uncle out and take over the place himself so that he could run it as a hotel?' The idea that Andrew would do such a callous thing was appalling. She stood up straight. 'You can't just throw someone out of their home. It's not that simple.'

'If he thinks so he's a fool,' said Michael.

She shivered. 'And we all know he isn't that. Misguided, but not a fool.' With another

89

glance at Zillah's cottage Michael bent to pick up his box of cyclamen.

CHAPTER EIGHT

Kathryn, standing at the kitchen door, could hardly believe that the day for the garden club visit had finally arrived. Already Zillah had placed her easel on the cobbled yard with a canvas on it ready for use outside her cottage. Several unframed paintings stood against the wall, their brilliant colours brightening a scene that Kathryn found appealing. She hoped the visitors would too.

They were due in just under an hour. In spite of Andrew's disapproval Sir Edwin wouldn't hear of cancelling the arrangement and Lady Hewson was quietly adamant that everything should go ahead as planned. They had not seen Andrew since.

Deep in thought, Kathryn turned away to check that the preparations were in order for the arrival of the visitors. All would be well as long as Andrew kept away. She had known early on that his apparent concern for his aunt and uncle's welfare was nothing but a sham. The deviousness of it was disturbing.

Obviously there was something deeper here than the trusting Hewsons were aware of and Michael thought so too. Her mother's job

90

would vanish for sure and she would lose the chance of living her dream. And herself? She sighed, ashamed of the split second relief she had felt at her mother's postponed return. She knew with deep certainty that to leave Bulbury Knap now would tear her into shreds.

And now there was the latest news of Zillah's burnt-out studio to worry about. Making the place habitable again and modernising the wiring, the likely cause of the fire, would take months. Kathryn felt a shimmer of doubt about the wisdom of Zillah's decision to ask Sir Edwin if she could stay on in the cottage permanently. If Andrew had plans for Bulbury Knap Zillah would be the first out and she didn't want that for her friend. Even if Andrew didn't get his way she wasn't quite sure that she liked the idea of having Zillah around all the time.

Kathryn sighed. So what did it make her . . . selfish and uncaring, that's what. Ashamed, she tried hard to be glad for Zillah that she had somewhere like this to stay.

Across the yard Zillah emerged from the cottage with another armful of paintings.

'What's this, a public exhibition?' Kathryn called across to her.

Zillah put her cargo down and waved. Her smock was ruffled and her dishevelled hair looked as if it hadn't seen a comb for weeks. 'Why not? I'll get changed in a minute and set to work. A bit of local colour.'

Kathryn walked across to her, smiling. 'Have you seen the display of cyclamen Michael's got ready in the greenhouse? Sir Edwin says they're impressive. All for sale. Other things too.'

'He's worked hard,' Zillah said. 'A great guy.'

'You've seen what Michael's been doing?'

'I've watched those flower buds unfurl as if they're my babies,' Zillah said lovingly.

There was something in her voice that made Kathryn pause. She hadn't seen much of Michael since meeting him in the yard a day or two ago. She had been busy too, of course, making batches of biscuits and sorting out a good recipe for the fruit punch that would be served today. She had picked up the hired glasses yesterday afternoon and Michael had helped unload them from the car on her return. He had organised the wine too but she had seen him only briefly on those occasions, understanding his need to get back to his own work. It seemed that Zillah had seen a lot more of him than she had.

Zillah finished placing her paintings against the wall. 'Michael reckoned it would be a good idea to have them on show,' she said. 'The boys say I'll sell them for thousands of pounds.' She gave a deep laugh. 'I told them that if I did Bulbury Knap would get twenty per cent commission.'

Kathryn smiled but her thoughts were

wandering to the impending visit. She had tried to make the dining room look less bare with large containers of laurustinus to hide the lack of furniture. Only the dining table had been undamaged and that would come into its own today for the serving of the fruit punch and nibbles. She hoped Andrew wasn't planning to drop in and put a dampener on things.

As soon as the visitors had started the tour of the garden Lady Hewson, her normally pale face flushed, sat down in a wicker chair and accepted the cup of coffee that Kathryn made for her. 'Thank you, dear. This is nice. I'll just drink this and then I'll help you clear up.'

Kathryn smiled. 'Please rest, Lady Hewson,' she said. 'You look exhausted.' She was piling coffee mugs on the tray as she spoke. 'I'll soon deal with these.'

Lady Hewson's cup rattled in the saucer. Kathryn leapt forward to catch it before it slithered to the floor. 'Lady Hewson . . .'

'I'm all right dear,' her employer murmured as she leaned back in her chair, eyes closed, and put her hand to her forehead.

Kathryn knelt at her side. 'Tell me what's wrong.'

'A little dizzy, that's all.' Lady Hewson opened her eyes and looked apologetically at Kathryn.

'I'll get Sir Edwin.'

'No, no, dear. Just a few minutes rest, that's

all. Nothing to worry about.'

Kathryn got to her feet, considering. But already the colour was returning to Lady Hewson's cheeks and Kathryn allowed herself to be convinced that it was a moment's tiredness only.

*   *   *

'You'll never believe it,' Zillah exclaimed. 'Five paintings sold and the promise of more orders over the phone. What d'you think of that?'

Kathryn looked at her friend's glowing face and smiled. 'That's wonderful, Zillah.'

'Unbelievable,' Zillah agreed. 'Nearly two hundred pounds commission for Bulbury Knap and more to come.'

Now Kathryn had a sudden idea. Bulbury Knap itself was the important issue here, for all of them. The Hewsons needed some good money-making schemes to be set up and this might well be one if Zillah agreed. She needed to think things through, though, and discuss them with Michael.

Euphoria at the success of the day set in later that evening. Even Lady Hewson, still a little pale, insisted on joining the others on the terrace outside the conservatory for a celebratory drink as dusk began to fall.

Michael, standing near Zillah's chair with a glass in his hand looked supremely content.

Kathryn supplied Tom and Neville with

glasses of fruit punch and indicated the plate of home-made biscuits on the stone table. She glanced across at the other two but hesitated to join them because they seemed engrossed in each other's company. Michael was seated now with his arm thrown casually across the back of Zillah's chair. Instead Kathryn chose to sit near Lady Hewson.

'Are you feeling better now?' she asked, bending forward a little. 'May I get you something more to drink?'

'No, dear. Not for the moment.' Lady Hewson's eyes were on her husband as he seated himself nearby. 'He's so happy,' she said fondly.

Kathryn smiled. It had been wonderful for them today, greeting old friends who came each spring to admire the gardens. She couldn't imagine the Hewsons being happy anywhere else. This was their life, their home of many years.

She thought of their daughter, Jane, far away in New Zealand whose home it had also been. Her e-mail address was interesting . . . jane@knap.com. Short and to the point. But didn't it show that Jane still felt herself part of the place where she had grown up? If, as she and Michael suspected, Andrew wanted Bulbury Knap for himself where would the kind Hewsons go to end their days?

'You look sad, dear,' said Lady Hewson.

'How can I be after such a successful day?'

she said.

'And much of it due to you, Kathryn.'

'All of us,' Kathryn said. 'We're a team.' She had a sudden glow round her heart at the thought of how well they had all worked together. Andrew's absence was one reason, of course. She wondered that he hadn't yet put in an appearance.

At last Michael left Zillah's side and made a move to leave the party in spite of loud protestations from his sons.

Sir Edwin got up, too. 'I think it would be wise for us to make a move inside, Dorothy, my dear,' he said, looking at her anxiously. 'It's been a long day.'

Kathryn felt tired too, now the excitement was over. Only Zillah seemed as full of life as ever, leaning back in her chair and waving a hand at Neville. 'Don't forget what we planned,' she said, winking at Tom. 'Come back to the cottage with me. I've got something to show you, Kathryn. You'll be surprised what I've been up to.'

The cottage door stood open and Zillah lead the way inside. At first Kathryn could see nothing but as her eyes became accustomed to the gloom she realised that a huge pile of canvasses stood against one wall.

'There,' said Zillah triumphantly. 'What do you think of these? I'd better light a candle,' Zillah said. 'Hang on a minute.'

By the flickering light Kathryn saw that each

canvas was a riot of glorious colour, in reds and oranges, yellows and purples. 'You've done all these in the last few days?' she was in wonder.

'This place inspires me,' Zillah said simply.

Even when she was back in the house making a start on the kitchen, Kathryn couldn't forget the exuberance of Zillah's work. Here was talent and plenty of it. Of course they must mount a special exhibition here at Bulbury Knap. She would talk to Michael about it in the morning.

The chance didn't come until the early evening because Michael had gone to Taunton on business for Sir Edwin and was away all day. There was no sign of Zillah as Kathryn set out to walk across the grass to Michael's cottage but she caught a glimpse of her red and purple smock as she walked up the garden path to the front door.

'Hi there, Kathryn,' Zillah called cheerfully from her stool amongst the azaleas. 'Aren't these beauties magnificent?'

Kathryn could see now where Zillah's inspiration came from. She stood behind her to gaze at the canvas on the easel, conscious of the sweet flower-scent on the evening air.

Zillah waved her brush. 'Michael's somewhere about. Give him a shout.'

He appeared at that moment, looking surprised to see Kathryn. For a moment she could say nothing, uneasy in case he thought she was spying on him.

'There's nothing wrong?' he asked.

She shook her head. 'I had an idea I wanted to talk through with you.'

'Then come inside. Though better still, why don't I bright us something to drink out here? Unless you want to talk privately?'

'It concerns Zillah too,' she said.

Zillah put down her brush, got up and stretched. 'Any excuse for a break.'

Michael was back in moments with a jug of lemonade and three glasses. They seated themselves on rickety garden chairs on the small patch of grass in the late sunshine.

'I've been thinking about arranging a special exhibition of Zillah's work at Bulbury Knap,' said Kathryn.

Zillah downed the last of her lemonade in a couple of gulps and the spluttered into her handkerchief, her eyes watering.

'The large room downstairs at the house would make a fine exhibition room,' Kathryn said, imagining it filled to overflowing with huge colourful paintings.

'We must go about it with care,' Michael said.

He hadn't seemed surprised at Kathryn's suggestion but she felt irked by his caution. She envisaged arranging good advertising, invitations sent to local art clubs, posters down in Lyme and other towns too, even the press invited.

'I'll have a word with Sir Edwin and see what he thinks,' he said.

She nodded. They would have to do that, of course. Her mind was obviously ahead of his. She looked hopefully at her friend. 'What do you think, Zillah?'

Zillah wiped her eyes and rammed her handkerchief back in her pocket. 'You'd do this for me?'

'And for Bulbury Knap,' said Michael. He gazed thoughtfully down at the glass in his hand. His usual stillness seemed to have intensified.

*   *   *

Kathryn knew that it was too much to hope that Andrew wouldn't get wind of their plans even though it was several days before Sir Edwin told him about it. Already many paintings had been hung and the publicity for the Bulbury Knap Open Day was in place.

Sir Edwin stood firm but Kathryn was horrified at Andrew's reaction though she kept well out of the way as Andrew stormed out of the house and strode off in the direction of the walled garden.

Afterwards, when Andrew had driven away in a fury, she sought out Michael and found him hoeing between lines of broad beans, a serious expression on his face. For a moment she watched him, unobserved. When he saw her he stopped what he was doing and stood leaning on his hoe.

She walked towards him. 'You've had a row with Andrew?' she said breathlessly.

'How are Sir Edwin and Lady Hewson now? I hope he hasn't upset them.'

'Surprised and a little shaken, I think. For goodness sake, why should Andrew mind the chance of an extra income for Bulbury Knap? I know this is a one-off but it could become a permanent thing in time. Very little work involved . . . except for Zillah of course, and she's loving it. Michael, there's something definitely odd about this.'

'I agree.'

'You said you have broadband,' she said abruptly. 'Could I ask a favour? I've thought about it carefully and I wanted to e-mail the Hewsons' daughter in New Zealand. I've written out what I want to say. Could you send it for me?'

He took the piece of paper she handed to him and read it. 'You've thought this through then?'

'I think Jane should be aware of what is going on. I believe it's a risk worth taking.' She looked at him steadily but it was impossible to gauge what he was thinking. At last he nodded. 'I'll do it now.'

CHAPTER NINE

Kathryn gazed out of the landing window at the branches of the oak tree against the metal-grey sky. A pigeon alighted and flew off again, spraying water on to the sodden grass beneath. As she watched, Zillah came striding across wearing a voluminous cape that almost hid the canvas she was carrying under one arm. Heading towards Michael's cottage . . . of course. More advice required, more details of the forthcoming open day to discuss?

She could see the two of them, heads together, as they worked out the final details that would make the day a resounding success. And that of course, was good. With a stab of pain Kathryn turned away, picked up her duster and attacked the windowsill as if it had done her a personal injury.

There, she was finished here now. Lady Hewson, down in the den, would be expecting her morning coffee and Sir Edwin would be in soon from whatever he was doing on the estate this wet morning.

On leaden feet she went down to the kitchen. Two days had passed since she had asked Michael to send the e-mail and by yesterday evening no reply had come. Maybe hers hadn't arrived in New Zealand. She could even have messed up the email address she'd given Michael. She had only glanced at it, after all, when Sir Edwin had given her the print-out to read. Anyone could have got it wrong.

Lady Hewson, a smile brightening her features, looked up from her embroidery as Kathryn carried in the tray to the den and placed it on the low table nearby. 'Such excellent news, dear. Jane is coming home to see us.'

Kathryn paused with the coffee pot in one hand, hope rising so swiftly she gasped. 'She is?'

'Andrew's had a long talk with her on the phone,' Lady Hewson said happily. 'We're so pleased.'

Carefully Kathryn poured Lady Hewson's coffee and handed her the cup and saucer. 'Of course you are, Lady Hewson,' she said as warmly as she could manage. So the risk she had taken in contacting Jane had misfired with a vengeance. Why hadn't she realised that Jane would be sure to contact Andrew on receiving her e-mail? No prizes for guessing what he had said to her.

'When will she be coming?' she asked.

'As soon as she can make the arrangements,' Lady Hewson said. 'Jane is so good at getting on with things once she has made up her mind.'

'Then I must sort out her room,' Kathryn said.

Lady Hewson's face clouded. 'Of course,

dear. I'd forgotten what the rooms are like now . . .' Her voice faded away.

Kathryn hurried up to the first landing, glad to have something practical to occupy her mind and stop her dwelling on the outcome of Jane's visit. She pushed open the bedroom door and looked at it in dismay. They had cleared the debris left after the thugs had done their worst and now it was empty apart from a single bed and a wardrobe.

She must do something at once . . . raid one of the other bedrooms whose curtains had not been touched, sort some bedding out from the linen cupboard and find a suitable chest of drawers from somewhere. If Jane took after either of her parents she would be the kind of person who liked pretty things. Later, she would pick some of the pink and white tulips from the front border and find something suitable to arrange them in.

*   *   *

Kathryn met Sir Edwin in the kitchen passage. Michael was with him. 'I've just heard that your daughter is coming home, Sir Edwin,' she said.

His eyes gleamed. 'So she is, my dear. And leaving my son-in-law to cope with the business on his own.'

She could see that Michael was already aware of this by the way he looked at her quizzically above his employer's head. Sir Edwin would have told him, of course. 'I need to have a word or two with Kathryn,' he said.

'A brief e-mail came this morning, short and to the point,' Michael said as he followed Kathryn into the kitchen and stood leaning against the closed door.

She could hardly bear to look at him for the rush of emotion that filled her throat. This was the man upon whom she had come to rely . . . the man who filled her thoughts day and night. Jane's ultimate decision about the future of Bulbury Knap would affect him deeply because he loved the garden and grounds here as if they were his own.

'What did she say?' she managed to get out.

'Arriving Bulbury Knap on Friday.'

'That's all?'

'Enough, wouldn't you say?'

She nodded. 'You know that she's been on the phone to Andrew?'

'That was only to be expected.'

She swallowed nervously. She hadn't thought of that in her haste to put Jane in the picture. How Michael must take her for a fool.

She caught his eye and smiled nervously. Just for a second his lips twitched in response. 'No doubt Andrew attempted to turn things to his advantage, but who knows the outcome? We'll have to wait and see.'

Michael was being so kind. Deeply she regretted her action but there was nothing she could do to help matters now. 'So she's coming on Friday, the day before the Open Day?' she said in a quiet voice.

'A good thing, wouldn't you say?'

'As long as we keep Sir Edwin and Lady Hewson out of it so they're not exhausted.'

'We will,' he promised. 'I've organised a couple of chaps from the village to take the money at the gate. Zillah's going to be stewarding the exhibition with the boys' help. They'll be handy for showing folk around the place, too. Refreshments in the conservatory, that's your province, and me in the walled garden area answering questions and manning the plant stall.'

'And Sir Edwin and Lady Hewson will be barricaded in the den?' she couldn't resist saying.

His lips twitched again and she smiled too, marvelling that they both could find amusement in this dire situation.

'We'll rely on Jane's presence to keep them away from too much of the action,' he said. 'She cares for her parents, Kathryn, or she wouldn't have dropped everything like this to come. She'll see how much they enjoy having people here and how much it all means to them.'

*   *   *

Her thoughts on Michael, Kathryn propped

105

open the back door to feel fresh air on her warm face. The rain had stopped now but the puddles on the cobbles reflected the leaden sky. Zillah's cottage door opened and Iain emerged, striding across to Kathryn with a cheerful wave.

'Iain!' It was good to see him even at this fraught moment. 'What brings you here?'

'To see you of course, dear Kathryn. And check on Zillah. She said I could come over the house to have a word.'

A split-second's thought that Zillah seemed to be taking over here at Bulbury Knap was quickly banished. Ashamed of herself, Kathryn smiled at him. 'I'm glad to see you, Iain,' she said.

'I've completed my research at last and now my book's ready to be written up.'

'That's great. You'll be able to give a hand with the Open Day. We could do with more help. Zillah's told you about it?'

'And given all the credit to you for coming up with the idea. You're quite a girl, Kathryn.' He slapped the leg of his ancient jeans. 'Not only that but I've been talking to the Lord of the Manor.'

'Sir Edwin?'

'The same. A decent old chap if I may say so.'

Kathryn saw the look of achievement on Iain's face. 'What have you been up to, Iain?'

'The old chap wanted to hear about the

106

research I've been doing. Seemed very knowledgeable about it. You know I've got myself in with the Heritage Centre people and I'm going to be doing a bit of work for them, a talk or two and help with the fossil hunts on the beach?'

'You haven't wasted much time.'

'Say you're pleased, Kathryn. It means a lot to me if you are.'

'Of course I'm pleased,' she said. 'You've worked so hard.'

'But?' He looked at her intently.

She tried to smile but her face felt stiff. Her mother's broken ankle was well on the mend now. Sarah had sounded so happy on the phone last night as she was beginning to make plans to take up her position at Bulbury Knap. It wouldn't be long now that her room in Polmerrick would become vacant again. Everything was shaping up.

Except for her, Kathryn, of course.

'You'll be able to return to Polmerrick now that Mum's better,' she said. He looked surprised. 'No way. Not with you here, Kathryn.'

'But I won't be here?' To her horror her voice trembled.

'Hey, hey, we can't have this.'

Suddenly his arms were round her and for a moment she leaned against him, grateful for his ready sympathy. He felt solid and comforting. 'We'll sort something out,' he said above her head.

She heard voices and pulled away, wiping her eyes on her sleeve. 'You're a good friend, Iain,' she murmured.

'More than that, I hope,' he said, his voice gruff. 'So this Open Day . . .'

'On Saturday.'

'I'll be here for you, Kathryn,' he promised.

*   *   *

'Andrew is making tea,' Lady Hewson said as if it was an every day occurrence. 'Your father will join us very soon, Jane, dear. And now here is Kathryn.'

Lady Hewson's face was flushed with pleasure as she introduced them. Jane was standing with her back to the light and Kathryn didn't notice at first that she had a scar running down her left cheek. She wondered that she didn't try to camouflage it but Jane's face was devoid of any makeup as far as she could see. They seated themselves at Lady Hewson's invitation in the wicker chairs that were placed in readiness on the terrace.

'This is nice,' said Lady Hewson.

Jane was older than Kathryn had imagined, a woman in her fifties with a stocky figure who gave the impression that any problem that reared its head would be dealt with firmly and at once. Her thick neck was almost hidden in the collar of her grey jersey and she wore a huge medallion on a solid chain. She leant confidently back in her chair that gave a little creak as she did so.

'And so, Kathryn, you've been making yourself at home,' she said in a deep voice that was oddly attractive.

Kathryn smiled, not quite knowing how to take the remark. 'Bulbury Knap is an easy place to do that,' she said.

'Too right.'

'And it's a pleasure to look after your parents.'

'I see.'

Lady Hewson leaned forward. 'What do you see, dear?'

At that moment Sir Edwin appeared, his stick tapping joyfully on the paving stones. Andrew, bearing a tray, followed him.

'Put it down there, my boy,' Sir Edwin said. 'I think Kathryn had better serve us all.'

Kathryn hesitated, looking at Lady Hewson to check whether she should proceed. As she said nothing she picked up the teapot and did as she was asked.

'And you've brought the chocolate biscuits,' Lady Hewson said with pleasure.

A self-deprecating smile touched one corner of Andrew's mouth. Obviously out to please, he had seated himself a little to the back of the group.

Kathryn finished serving everyone and Andrew gave her a nod of dismissal. She caught a look of surprise on Jane's face as she turned to go but Jane said nothing. Of course this was the moment for some serious talking and Kathryn was not to be part of it.

*   *   *

This time there wasn't the sudden advent of people on the day that Bulbury Knap was thrown open to the general public but rather a slow trickle spread over the whole time.

Kathryn sank into one of the wicker chairs in the conservatory, too weary to think of finding the others for the moment. She had seen little of Jane all day because Andrew had made himself responsible for escorting her from one place to another, no doubt wanting her to see it all from his point of view.

But Jane couldn't fail to have seen the enjoyment of the people who came and how they thronged into Zillah's exhibition. She knew the takings for this were well up because Iain, who came to help, told her so.

But was the price too high for Sir Edwin and Lady Hewson? She had caught a glimpse of Sir Edwin at one point, leaning on his stick as he beheld the crowds wandering in his grounds, his old face suffused with pride. Iain had come up to him at that moment and helped him to a seat on the terrace beside his wife. She had also seen Jane with her mother who lay back in one of the reclining seats with

110

her eyes closed.

Now Kathryn looked up and Michael was there. His face looked drawn and his eyes weary. He sank down on the padded window. She longed to comfort him, to sit close and draw his head down on her shoulders and take some of the burden from him.

'I've been talking to Jane,' he said, his voice flat. 'She's made an appointment to come to see me at the cottage in half an hour. I thought you should know. It doesn't sound good.'

Her mouth dry, Kathryn stared at him in dismay as he got to his feet. She watched him go with deep foreboding in her heart.

CHAPTER TEN

Lady Hewson kept to her room next morning, tended by her daughter who emerged at coffee time looking far from happy. She had changed her grey jersey today for an orange one but was still wearing the medallion on its thick chain.

Kathryn had prepared a tray and was about to take it up when she found Jane in the hall.

'I'll take it up to my mother and be right back,' Jane said. 'No coffee for me. I don't drink it.'

Yesterday Jane had seen the exhaustion of both her parents. How could she not be concerned that Bulbury Knap was now too much for them, however much help was at hand?

'Come into the den. We need to talk,' Jane said when she returned.

The room was cold and Kathryn shivered a little. 'How is Lady Hewson?' she asked.

Jane shrugged and sat down. 'It's crazy to think that she can stay on here in her state,' Jane said in her abrupt manner. 'My father, too. He's not fit to be let loose on the estate.'

'Oh but . . .' Kathryn started to remonstrate but then stopped at a wave of Jane's hand. It was not her place to argue after all. Jane had already had a long session with Michael who would have been totally honest. Michael and Zillah would have plans of their own. Her mother would find other employment, Helen would have her baby down in Cornwall, she herself would go away back to her old life in London, teaching . . . Bulbury Knap would seem like a dream. Michael . . .

'Are you all right?' Jane asked in concern.

With a supreme effort Kathryn smiled. 'It's so sad.'

'They should be rid of this place,' Jane said with conviction. 'I've no children to be considered and my home's in New Zealand now and always will be. What would you have me do? Let my parents moulder on here until they give up the ghost?'

'So what will happen now?' Kathryn asked

112

humbly.

'I've had Michael's input and now I need yours, Kathryn,' Jane said, leaning forward. 'They're fond of you and I know you'll be fair. Tell me all of the instances where you have been most concerned about my parents.'

It was no use trying to hide anything but it was hard to come out with the occasions that had caused worry knowing that it must result in Sir Edwin and Lady Hewson being forced to leave their home. 'If Andrew takes over Bulbury Knap what will happen to your parents?' Kathryn asked at last.

'I'll get them moved into something smaller.'

'On the estate?'

'Maybe.'

Kathryn could think only of one property that was even remotely suitable . . . Michael's cottage. Horrified, she gazed at Jane. Michael and his boys homeless . . . she couldn't bear the thought of him having to uproot his little family, to move away to find work elsewhere, away from the place he loved, the garden he had poured such love and attention into.

'On the other hand I'm open to all ideas,' Jane said. 'It won't happen overnight but I have to consider the welfare of my parents.'

Kathryn appreciated that Jane was being reasonable but as she returned to the kitchen to start preparing lunch she couldn't help thinking of her own mother's deep

113

disappointment if her job at Bulbury Knap was no longer open to her.

The back door burst open and Zillah was in the doorway, looking supremely confident in her purple and magenta smock. 'Come on Kathryn. It might never happen.'

Kathryn smiled weakly. If only she could be sure of that.

'I'm off to see Michael,' Zillah said. 'I've a plan to hatch that'll solve all our problems.'

*　　*　　*

Sarah's phone call that evening came as something of a relief to Kathryn. She had been putting off her mother but now she had no choice but to warn her of the latest developments at Bulbury Knap.

Afterwards she marvelled at Sarah's reaction . . . initial disappointment, of course, but then deep concern for the Hewsons and for Kathryn herself.

'Don't worry about me,' Kathryn had said, tight-lipped. 'I'll find something. I'm a free agent. I can go anywhere.'

But she didn't want to go anywhere. She put down the receiver and stood with her head against the wall, unable for the moment to think of what to do next. Andrew and Jane were closeted in his study upstairs and had been there for some time. Finalising details of Andrew's take-over, she supposed. She wondered that Jane would condone the plans Andrew obviously had for Bulbury Knap that would render it totally unrecognisable from the beloved family home it had been for generations.

*   *   *

Kathryn was awakened suddenly by the banging of doors, the crash of footsteps. She sat up in bed, heart thudding. Then she slipped on her dressing-gown and slippers and opened her bedroom door. Up here on the top floor she felt cut off from the rest of the house but she needed to know what was going on in the dead of night. She switched on the landing light and stood listening.

Not a sound now. Had she dreamt the noise she had heard earlier? She went down to the first floor landing, stepping gingerly so as not to make any noise herself. Then she stood still, listening to the silence. She must have imagined the racket that had seemed to shake the house, the tail end of a nightmare perhaps now mercifully forgotten.

She went down to the kitchen with the intention of making herself a drink. To her alarm the front door stood open. For the first time she remembered the intruders who had raided the place all those weeks ago. The hall felt icy as she rushed to the door to close and lock it. She felt safer now but this was stupid.

Anyone with any sense would have awakened someone . . . Andrew or Jane, not descended into goodness knows what danger on her own.

She stood, wondering what to do, and then heard a car starting up outside, tyres on the gravel, the roar as it went off and then heavy silence again.

With a spurt of energy she bounded up to the first floor landing and tapped on Jane's door. Even as Jane's strong voice bid her enter Kathryn knew that the car was Andrew's.

Bemused, she stared at the older woman. Jane, dressed in outdoor clothes, was seated on her bed with a laptop beside her looking as if this was perfectly reasonable in the middle of the night.

'I heard a noise,' Kathryn said.

'Andrew departing,' said Jane calmly. 'Did he alarm you?'

'I thought I should check.'

Jane nodded. 'He'll be back. He's not finished with me yet.'

'Can I get you anything?'

'Not a thing. Get back to bed, my dear. Sorry you were disturbed.'

For the rest of the night Kathryn's sleep was troubled and she awoke in the morning with the consciousness that momentous decisions had already been made that Andrew was not pleased about.

Breakfast was late because Jane didn't emerge from her room until nearly ten o'clock.

Kathryn served Sir Edwin and Lady Hewson at their usual time and settled them in the den with a fresh pot of tea and the morning newspapers for Sir Edwin and her embroidery for Lady Hewson.

Jane ate her meal in a silence that was heavy with foreboding. This seemed to deepen as Andrew came in and sat down at the place at the kitchen table Kathryn had laid for him. His dark hair was slightly tousled and his blue open-necked shirt had the top button missing.

He ate absently, then pushed his plate away and got up to stride to the window and then back again. As he sat there with one leg hitched over the arm of his chair Kathryn wasn't sure how much she really disliked him any more. She could have felt sorry for him if there hadn't been so much at stake. It was clear that he had met his match in Jane.

Kathryn found plenty to occupy her during the day with the clearing up of the conservatory. China to replace in its usual home and checking that all was well with the rest of the house that was her preserve. Zillah didn't seek her out and Michael was nowhere to be seen. Jane phoned for a taxi and was away until early evening. Sir Edwin and Lady Hewson, pathetically grateful for the simple meals she served them, insisted that Kathryn rested during the afternoon and left them to their own devices.

Left to her own devices, Kathryn wandered

from room to room unable to settle to anything. Gradually she became aware that the sky was darkening. She glanced anxiously out of the front door and saw her employers nearby admiring the purple clematis on the wall. They came immediately they saw her, glad to be settled in the den after their walk.

Much later, after the evening meal had been cleared and Jane and her parents closeted together for a long talk, Kathryn let herself out of the back door for a breath of fresh air. As yet the rain that had threatened all afternoon had come to nothing but there was an ominous feeling to the evening that fitted in well with her mood. Zillah's door was closed but a flickering light shone from the window.

Not wanting to disturb her, Kathryn hurried by and by the time she reached the expanse of lawn that led down to the lake, she was beginning to come to terms with how things were going to be.

Her heart heavy, Kathryn reached the lakeside and stood beneath the swaying trees to gaze out across the ruffled water. She had been down here several times since that evening when Michael had joined her but the memories of that were still painful. Had he brought Zillah here on calm evenings since that magic time?

She sighed, regretting her impulse to pull away from his embrace when, even then, she had recognised the perfect moment. Now it was too late. She had thought about it so often, changing the scenario in her mind so that sometimes it seemed as if it had really happened.

She would have to leave Bulbury Knap and, in the circumstances, the sooner the better. What good was she here now that her mother's job was no longer open to her and Jane was present to tend her parents' needs? She should follow Sarah's example and accept the future with good grace knowing that the pain of seeing Michael and Zillah together could be eased only by her absence from the scene.

She was conscious now that rain was falling, pitting the surface of the lake. Raising her face, she felt the drips from the overhanging branches caress her face, resolving to tell the Hewsons when she got back, promise to stay on for a week or two to help them pack and then go down to Cornwall to see her own family before deciding where she should make her future. At the moment she longed only to be far away from Bulbury Knap.

The rain was harder now and in the distance thunder rumbled. Uncaring, she stayed where she was until the fierceness of the drops had soaked her hair and clothes. Even then she was reluctant to move away from the comparative shelter of the trees. What did anything matter now when everything she had hoped for when she first arrived was now in shatters?

A blaze of lightning sheeted across the sky followed by an explosion of thunder and lashing hailstones. Head down, she turned and ran for Michael's cottage.

The path was awash and she stumbled through the water to hammer on the door. He opened it immediately.

She almost fell inside as a deafening crack split the heavens in two, followed by a crash of smashing branches beyond the garden gate.

'A tree's down,' Michael said, slamming the door shut behind her. 'You could have been killed. What d'you think you're doing out in this?' His anger was palpable in the stormy air.

She stood gasping, water streaming from her hair and her clothes. 'I'll go, I'll get back to the house . . .'

'You most certainly won't,' he said, his voice stern. And she didn't wonder, faced with a desperate apparition dripping water over the flagstones of his hallway.

'Wait there,' he ordered and was back immediately with a huge bath sheet. 'Get the worst wiped off with this. Come on, it won't bite.'

She wiped her face, scrubbed at her hair and then held the towel round her body to soak some of the moisture from her sweatshirt and jeans, kicking off her shoes. She looked, disbelieving, though the living-room doorway. Where were the cushions, the photographs, the carpet . . . the scent of furniture polish that had enchanted her on her last visit? Now the room was bare of ornaments and on the floorboards stood three large boxes, one of them overflowing with folded curtains.

Outside the rain lashed the window and the sky was black but the thunder had faded away to a low rumble.

'The boys . . .' she whispered.

'At Mrs Pearce's for the night while I do a bit of packing,' he said with a calmness that alarmed her.

'You're going then?' All at once it was too much . . . Jane's decision for her parents, the storm, Michael leaving . . . lost to her for ever though he was lost to her already . . . Bulbury Knap . . .

'I must go,' she said in desperation. 'I've no business here.'

'I'm ahead of myself,' he said. 'There's plenty of time to move out. I just seized the opportunity with the boys away for the night.'

'Where will you go?'

He looked surprised. 'You don't know?'

How could she know? How could she know anything more? She turned to leave, in her haste forgetting the towel wrapped round her. She tripped and would have fallen if Michael hadn't grabbed her.

'I'm all right,' she whispered, pulling free.

'No way. You're staying here and getting into something warm. The bathroom's at the back and there's hot water for a shower. I'll find something for you to wear.'

In the shower she held her face up to the water, letting it mingle with weak tears. The clothes he had given her were some of Tom's he had yet to grow into and she was grateful for their comfort.

She pulled the polo neck of the Aran jersey high up her neck and rolled the cuffs back. Then, still barefooted, she gathered up her own wet clothes and joined him in the kitchen.

'That's better,' he said with approval. 'I've phoned the house to say where you are. I'll get the car out later and run you back. First though, I'll get the kettle on.'

He soon had it organised. Her face glowed though she was frozen inside from knowing this was the end. When Michael finished his tea and shrugged himself into his thick jacket she watched numbly. A blast of wind almost took the door out of his hand. 'It's stopped raining,' he said.

He was back almost immediately, shrugging off his jacket. 'No go,' he said. 'The lane's blocked with the fallen tree. Nothing doing till the morning. My bed's been changed and I'll doss down in the boy's room.'

'No, no. I'll walk. I'll climb over the tree. I'll . . .' she was on her feet now staring at him wildly. 'I . . . I can't.'

'I'll get the fire going in the other room. Come on.'

There was a pile of grey blankets in one

corner and he spread them on the bare boards in front of the glowing flames.

She sank down and held her cold hands to the warmth, wanting to go and yet wanting to be here near him too.

'Remember fitting out Zillah's cottage before she moved in?' he said, sinking down beside her.

'Zillah,' she whispered.

'An asset to the place if ever there was one. Just shows how bad things can change to good, for Bulbury Knap and the for the boys and me.'

She nodded, unable to speak for the pain that tore at her. Instead she caught hold of the edge of a blanket and twisted the edge.

'And I have you to thank, Kathryn, for the way things have slotted into place,' he said.

'Me?'

'Zillah came to Bulbury Knap because of you.'

Kathryn was silent, aware she had done Michael a great service. She loved him. She should be proud of the part she had played in his future happiness. She had already seen that his packing up to leave the cottage was not the catastrophe she had imagined because he had found Zillah.

He reached forward to throw another log on the fire. The flames hissed a little, died down and then flamed up again. 'And it was your efforts, Kathryn, on behalf of Zillah that inspired me to suggest that Bulbury Knap becomes a residential centre for the arts.'

Kathryn clutched at the edge of the blanket and then let it go. 'But Andrew . . . ?'

He smiled, his eyes warm. 'Andrew doesn't come into it any more. He and Jane had the bust up to end all bust ups. She could see the way things were going and didn't fall for his scheming to buy the place at a knockdown price. She's got a head on her shoulders, that one. She liked the idea of the art centre at once and did a bit of research yesterday and today, enough to know that it's viable.

'Zillah was central to this, of course. You might have noticed that I've been seeing a lot of Zillah lately. That's why. Jane made me keep it under wraps until she got back from Taunton today. It's a wonder Zillah suspected nothing. A great girl but a touch naive. Now you, Kathryn, would have caught on at once.'

Kate stared at him uncomprehendingly. 'But I don't understand.'

'It was all a necessary part of the procedure,' he said. 'I had to make sure Zillah would be willing to tutor art classes as well as hold her own exhibitions here. And she can. Sir Edwin wants to arrange for your friend to be a tutor too.'

'My friend?'

'The Jurassic coast man. Could you ask him? Accommodation will be provided for him, of course, in the cottage next to Zillah.'

124

'And you?'

'Garden design,' he said proudly. 'Week-long courses for about ten students at a time. This is something I've long wanted to do. We can still take the garden club visits every summer. Sir Edwin is pleased about that.'

'So he and Lady Hewson can still live in the house?'

Michael shook his head. 'Can you imagine it with the place bustling with enthusiastic students? No, this cottage will be converted into a home for them with your mother looking after them as well as overseeing the house. Accommodation will be provided for her there.'

Relief flooded over her. 'You mean, my mother will still have her job here?'

'Of course. She'll be needed now more than ever.'

'That's wonderful,' said Kathryn, still hardly able to believe it. 'And me?' she added. 'What use will I be?'

For answer Michael leaned towards her and pulled her close. 'You are pivotal to the whole scheme as the manager,' he said gently. 'And especially pivotal to me.'

She trembled in his arms as he kissed her, leaning into his warmth. Everything seemed to happen in slow motion and at the same time swiftly as the wind.

'I want you by my side for the rest of our lives,' he said, his voice husky. 'It's my dearest wish, Kathryn, my love.'

She couldn't speak because he kissed her again. This time there could be no doubt in his mind that it was her dearest wish, too.

Kathryn glanced at the box of brilliant pink cyclamen Michael had placed at his feet on the cobbled yard as she emerged from the kitchen for a few minutes restorative air this bright February morning. She paused, surprised to see Michael so smartly dressed at this time of day.

'What gorgeous colours,' she said 'Are they for the sale?'

He nodded. 'Lady Rennie is fond of them. She wants the place to look welcoming for the .... Club .... tomorrow. I thought I'd bring some up to Zillah at the same time to brighten up the cottage. I know she likes them.'

'You do?'

Michael gazed down at the flowers, still pursing his lips. His white shirt gleamed in the sunshine and his jeans looked new.

'Zillah's .... Djust at the moment, Michael.'

He looked disappointed. 'I'll leave it outside her door then.' He made to pick up the box again but then hesitated, as if suddenly remembering something. 'So, how's it going then, Kathryn? With Andrew, I mean.'

She sighed. 'I can't take much more of everything, she ...... But .... cold and polite. What's he playing at, Michael?'

He frowned. 'Some devious plan, afoot, I

Kathryn walked across to her, smiling. 'Have you seen the display of cyclamen Michael's got ready in the greenhouse? Sir Edwin says they're impressive. All for sale. Other things too.'

'He's worked hard,' Zillah said. 'A great guy.'

'You've seen what Michael's been doing?'

'I've watched those flower buds unfurl as if they're my babies,' Zillah said though a ...

There was something in her voice that made Kathryn pause. She hadn't seen much of Michael since meeting him in the pub a day or two ago. She had been busy, of course, making lunches in the cafe. She had arrived in a good temper for the first period but would be served today. She had picked up the aprons, glasses yesterday afternoon, and Michael had helped unload them from the car on her return. He had returned the wine too, but she had seen him only briefly on those occasions, understanding his need to get back to his own work. It seemed that Zillah had seen a lot more of him than she had.

Zillah finished placing her paintings against the wall. 'Michael reckoned it would be a good idea to have them on show,' she said. 'The boys say I'll sell them for thousands of pounds.' She gave a deep laugh. 'I told them that if Julia Bulbury was in, she would get twenty per cent commission.'

Kathryn smiled but her thoughts were

92